SCANDALS
OF A *CHI-TOWN*
THUG

SCANDALS
OF A *CHI-TOWN*
THUG

By

J.J. Jackson

Felony Books, a division of Olive Group, LLC,
P.O. Box 1577, Belton, MO 64012

ISBN-13: 978-1546370710

Felony Books 1st edition May 2017

10 9 8 7 6 5 4 3 2

Manufactured in the United States of America

For information regarding special discounts for bulk purchases, please contact Felony Books at felonybooks@gmail.com.

Dedication Page

I would like to thank the universe first, for all it is doing for me to bring me my heart's desire. I would also like to thank God for giving me the courage, strength and know-how. I would also like to thank my mom for being who she is and for putting up with all of me. Mom, without you, I would not be.

To my prison family, and all the readers in the United States and overseas, I would like to say thank you for all you do for me as I walk this thin line day after day. It is a hard walk, but I get through it because of all of you being there to support me. It means so much to me knowing that there are people like you showing me love day after day.

To all the families that have lost someone to the streets, my heart and prayers go out to you. May your loved one/ones rest in peace. And to the families that have lost someone to this hardcore penal system, hang in there, your change will come. Believe that this too shall pass.

This novel is dedicated also to all the real Gangsters; not the RATS, but the Gangsters.

One real Gangster said:

"Time is of the essence. Yesterday is history. Tomorrow is a mystery. Today is not promised, it's a gift. People, it's all about right now. Cherish each moment of every day as if it's your last. Live in the moment because time is of the essence." Quoted by Peter Shue. Get his story: *The Peter Shue Story: The life of the Party!* His story is the real deal!

To all walks of life, if you are going through any adversities remember to keep your head up and Live!!!

LUV Y'ALL!

CHAPTER 1

"Put your hands on the car, I said."

"Why man? I ain't do shit, why you fuckin wit me?!"

"Man, if you don't put yo fuckin' hands on the car I'ma put two in you!" the officer says as he points a 9mm at Mr. Andre Smalls.

"Man, this some real bull shit, man. I say I ain't do shit!"

The backup officers pull up on the scene. A really muscle bound officer jumps out of the car. He tackles Mr. Smalls to the ground.

"What's going on here?" another officer asks.

"This piece of shit almost ran me over as he ran the stop light back there, so I pulled him over. And when I asked him for his license he told me to fuck off 'cause he ain't do shit," he explains.

"Did you check the car?"

"No, he wouldn't even put his hands on the car."

The officer pops Mr. Smalls's trunk.

"Oh shit! Oh Shit!" The officer jumps back. The first officer runs over to see what's going on.

"What the fuck is going on here? A fucking body! Run it and see who he is, and if anybody has reported a missing person." Officer Mills makes his way to Mr. Smalls, who is handcuffed, laying face down on the cold wet ground.

"Who is he?"

"Who is who?" he says.

"The body in the car?"

"What body in what car? I'on know what you talking about."

"So you gon' play dumb, huh?"

"No, I just don't know what you're talking about."

Wack!

"*Ahhhhh* shit!"

Officer Mills just hit him in his face with the butt of his gun."

"Does that jog your memo, you piece of shit? Book his ass. I want to know all about'em. I want this muthafucka to pay, y'all hear me? I want his blood!" Office Mills yells out.

They put him in the car.

Andre is so mad at himself. *I knew I should have left his ass at the house. Man, some'em told my black ass to leave him. Shit, this is a bad day man, this is not good at all. How I'm gon' get out this shit? Who the fuck can I call for this?* he thinks to himself, as he watches all the squad cars pull up to the scene.

CHAPTER 2

"G, I'on know 'bout you, I'm sick of flippin' these burgers," Ray lets out while grilling some hamburger meat on his job at Mr. Roy Rogers.

"Yeah, I feel you on that there. It's like we went through high school, did all that learning, graduated, and now look at us. We working for Mr. Rogers," Bruce expresses, lowering the frozen fries into the bubbling grease of the oversized deep fryer.

"Welcome to Mr. Roy Rogers. May I take your order?" the young cashier asks the man who's standing in front of her.

Ray looks up. "G, look. Look at that nigga. He fresh ta deaf as always. Look at that freakin' watch! The joint is iced the fuck out!" Ray says excitedly.

"I see, man. That's Youngbleed for you ... he be slingin' them rocks, I hear," Bruce lets out, while still cooking fries.

"G, that there is how I wanna be livin'. Look at his fuckin' whip! That joint sittin' on fo' fo's," he marvels. Ray is so outdone over Youngbleed, he doesn't notice his burgers are burning.

"Ray! Ray, what you doing man! My burgers son, they're burning!" the manager shouts, running over to the grill.

"Oh shit!" Ray snaps out of his trance and flips the burgers over as fast as he can. Bruce starts laughing.

"So you think that's funny? That's four burgers, and that my son is coming outta yo boy Ray's pay," his manager explodes.

"C'mon, man. I'on make shit as it is," Ray protests.

"And if you keep burning my meat, you won't be making shit else. Yo ass will be jobless," old man Roger walks up to Ray and says.

Ray looks at Bruce, who throws his hands up.

"Well ... go get some more burgers!" the old man orders him.

Ray walks to the back of the fast food restaurant, opens the freezer when a thought pops into his head. He freezes and then a smile cracks his face.

"Yeah, that's what I'ma do. I'ma be rich, rich, rich just like my brother was and Youngbleed is," he verbalizes out loud to himself as he closes the freezer door and heads back to his station.

CHAPTER 3

Mr. Smalls sits in a room at the Chicago police department. Mr. Mack, the head detective, walks in.

"Mr. Smalls, how are you today?" he asks.

"I'm Gucci, in spite of," Mr. Smalls says, keeping cool as he can.

"Would you like some coffee, soda or anything?"

"Nah, like I just said I'm Gucci."

"Ok, let's get down to it. Mr. Smalls, so you're telling us that you never seen the car that officer William pulled you over in? 'Cause in the truck he's saying he found a dead man—a dead *young* man—and you're stating you don't know who that man is. Is this all correct, Mr. Smalls?" The Detective reads from a paper that's in a brown folder laying on the table before him.

Poogie looks the detective in his eyes. "Man, I'm not sayin' shit until my lawyer get here!"

"Until your lawyer gets here? Mr. Smalls, to be frank with you it don't matter how many lawyers you have. See, we have you driving the car. We have the body that was found in the back of the car you were driving. So how much more do you think we need to put you away for life? Oh yeah, did I forget the loaded gun we found in the hidden compartment of that car you know nothing about? Now Mr. Smalls, I'm sure the ballistics from that gun will match the bullet wounds in the head of the deceased young man. One more thing I need to inform you about: we ran the plates and you can only guess whose name they came back in. Now tell me what lawyer do you have?"

"Excuse me, I need to confer with my client." A tall white man enters the interrogation room, cutting Detective Mack off.

"That lawyer right there," Poogie spits with a smile across his face as he answers the Detective's last question. "What took you so damn long?" Poogie asks Attorney Wellcock, one of the most prominent Attorneys in Chicago.

"I got held up in traffic."

The Detective excuses himself as he eyes Mr. Wellcock and exits the room. They have a lot of respect for Mr. Wellcock.

Mr. Wellcock turns his attention to his client. "So what did you go and get yourself into now?"

"Man, I fucked up. I really fucked up. This nigga owe me some bread and he was giving me the run around so I called him and told him I was gon' leave him a big message if he'in turn up wit my bread by 8 that night. I told him where to meet me but he'in show his face, so I did what had to be done."

"And what might that be, Smalls?" his lawyer asks with his hands folded on the table. Smalls positioned across from his lawyer.

"I went to his baby mommy house, fucked her brains out, strangled the bitch, then put one in her eye to seal the deal."

"Did you rape her?"

"Hell naw, she gave it to me willingly. I would never rape nobody, *please*. Her pussy wasn't worth that shit. It was a'ight."

"Any children?" Wellcock asks, looking in Mr. Smalls's eyes.

"Look man, that shit don't madda. Can you get me off?"

"No, not if your semen is in her and you had the weapon with you. Now what about the young man they found in the truck of the car you were driving?"

"Oh yeah, the body ... that was her man. He was an added bonus."

"An added bonus?" the attorney repeats, lowering his reading glasses.

"Yeah, that nigga was coming up the drive when I was leaving. I asked that punk ass bitch nigga where my money? He was like, 'Fuck you nigga, fuck you doing here fo?' That was all she wrote. I put one in his face, then in his head, sending his ass to meet his maker, then I stuffed him in my truck. I was gon' drop his ass off at his peeps' house. I hate they assess, they did some real sticky shit to me some days ago."

"Really?"

"G, what can you get me if you I ain't beatin' this shit?"

"What do you have?" Wellcock looked at him with a serious face. "What do you have? What can you give them that will set you free?"

Mr. Smalls sits up in his chair, leans across the table. "You mean rat on somebody?"

"That's what I mean," he answers quickly.

"Nah, I can't do dat. Hell nah man, you trippin'."

"Well, you will spend 15 to life in prison. Your life, your choice."

"But you're my lawyer."

"Yes, I'm your lawyer, not God. So *pray,*" he tells him, gathering his papers.

"But I'm paying you eighty bones! What dat get a nigga? Sho nuff not life I know!" Poogie spits with venom.

"Yes you are paying me eighty thousand dollars, and it will be more than that if we have to go to trial."

"Wait! How about I give them some dirty cops," Poogie says, crossing his arms across his chest, now rocking his chair on its back legs.

"That's a start. But that won't get you much time off," Wellcock informs him.

"Man, I just can't be a rat nigga. Dat shit is going against the code."

"Well, I don't see none of them code people around you about now, and they're not going to do the time, you are. Let me talk to the detective that is handling your case. I'll see if he wants to negotiate."

"That sounds like a winner to me."

Mr. Wellcock leaves the room and returns within 30 minutes alone.

"Ok, they are willing to work something out but they're going to need something more than dirty cops. They want drug dealers. They want bodies."

"Shit, dis here is fucked up. Man ok, ok. How about I give them this cat I know who is selling drugs on a low scale."

"Now you know they want something bigger than that," his lawyer tells him.

Poogie lays his head on the table. "Man shit, I'll do it. I can't do life, I just can't do life. I'm a rat. Shit." He lifts his head, looks at his lawyer. "Ok, I know this cat who murdered these niggas. And I can give them a drug bust. But I can't give it to them all at once 'cause it will look funny. Feel me?"

"I do," the lawyer says, patting him on his shoulder as if he's the detective now.

After that, an FBI agents walk in the room. He looks over at Poogie's lawyer, then at Poogie. He takes a seat at the table.

"I will not lie, I heard most of what the two of you were saying and this is my offer, Mr. Smalls. We want you to work for us. If you take the offer, everything you did will no longer be a worry in your life," he tells him, clicking his pin. "You will only have to do one year for the gun."

"One year if I work for y'all? What the fuck?"

"It beats life, because that's what we'll go for," the Agent tells him.

"What's your name? Who are you?" Poogie asks.

"Oh I'm sorry. I'm agent Leon from the FBI."

"The FBI? What happened to state?"

"When you drove the body across state lines, it became a federal case," Agent Leon explains.

"Ok, I'll do it but I want all of this in black and white … that's funny, black and white," Poogie says, looking at his lawyer, the agent, and then the Detective who are all white.

"Mr. Smalls, this is the smartest move you've ever made. You're saving money on a trial and you're saving your life," his lawyer assures.

CHAPTER 4

"It's hotta than a bitch's pussy out this mug! Hell, I think the sun is mad as hell at us black niggas," Poogie spits while sitting on the steps with his boys in one of the toughest projects in Chicago, The Wild Hunnids.

"G, you ain't neva lied 'bout that shit. I hate the summer. It be all sticky, all these fuckin' bugs. I mean really?" Shorty Duce intervenes, swatting the flies away from his face. "Who thought of fuckin' flies and shit? Why they even here?" he continues to complain.

"Fuck what y'all niggas heard. I love the summer, G. That's when all the bunnies start hoppin' and I love 'em all," one of his boys joins the convo.

"Whateva, G. You'on even get no coudie. You'on even know what that shit smells like," Poogie clowns. All of them start laughing.

"You say G, but I still say I love them summer freaks."

"I guess you do. At least you get ta look ... if nothin' else. A nigga can dream," Shorty Duce clowns him as well. They all continue to down their beers and clown around until Youngbleed pulls up in his black Range Rover.

Kim opens the passenger door and steps out. She's sexy with long black hair, black eyes, long legs, and a home-made phat ass with homemade triple F breasts to match. Her complexion is brown, her skin is flawless, thanks to the tanning booth that she hits up every weekend. She shuts the door, works what she got across the street, paying the block niggas no mind.

"Damn, that's one fine bitch! I knew I should've hit that back in high school when I had the chance!" Shorty Duce screams.

"G, back in high school? Hell you talk like that shit was years ago. You just graduated last fuckin' year!" Poogie reminds him, still clowning around.

"Fuck you, nigga. The fact remains I could've hit," he shoots back.

"Nigga, you wish. Yo ass too broke to hit shit. That bitch is high maintenance. She ain't 'bout ta fuck wit no broke as nigga," Poogie continues through the laughter.

"That you right about, my man. That's why a nigga gotta get this paper right. And when I do, I'm gunnin' for'a," Shorty Duce says with a serious tone.

"Yo, G! Snap out that dumb shit and hand me another cold one out that there cooler," Poogie tells him having thoughts of his own.

CHAPTER 5

Bloc! Bloc! Bloc!

These are the sounds that wake Bruce from his sleep.

"Man, I'm tired of this shit, waking up to gunshots all the damn time. I gotta get out this fuckin' hood!" Bruce whines, while climbing out of bed. Just as his feet hit the cold concrete floor, he looks over at the clock.

"Ten in the morning and all these niggas know is gun smoke. Shit!" he rants on as he walks to the bathroom.

Smash!

"Fuckin' roaches! I hate 'em. Man, it's hot as hell in here!" he continues to whine while taking a piss and shaking his penis over the toilet. He looks at himself in the mirror, washes his hands, and then brushes his teeth.

"Ma, ma," he calls out, walking down the long hallway to the living room of his mother's apartment. "Is the air conditioners broke?" he asks her.

"No boy, you know I don't like that stale air. I like the window open and the fans blowing. See, when I was young we ain't have no air conditioners," she tells him from the kitchen in her blue and white flower cotton nightgown.

"Yeah, yeah, yeah ... I know ma, but you ain't young now and we do have air in the window for a reason, so can we turn it on?"

"Now BJ, you have one in your window in your room so you can go in there and turn it on and you will have all the air you like. But since this is my place and you live in it, I choose where the air blows. You know I'm 65 now and that air gets in my bones," Bruce's grandmother explains while cooking bacon, eggs, and toast for breakfast.

Bruce's mother OD'd when he was in ninth grade and he never knew his father. Bruce and his mother had been living with his grandmother since he was knee high. He has always called his grandmother "Ma" because his mother was never home for him to get to know her.

"Did you get any letters from them colleges, boy?"

"Yeah, I'm still deciding which one I want to go to."

"Well another sports agent called. I think he's from NCU."

"NCU, huh?"

"Yeah, that's what I said. Now ain't that a good one you can go to? You done turned your nose up at so many of 'em. Soon you ain't gon' have one to pick. They gon' stop calling for ya. You gon' have ta pick one so you can get outta these here projects. Make some'em of your life," she tells him, turning from the stove placing the food on the table in front of him. She notices Bruce is lost in thought. "What is it, son? What's going on in that head of yours?"

"Nuttin', Ma. Nuttin' at all," he mumbles.

"Boy, don't you lie to me," she continues. "I can see it in yo eyes."

He locks eyes with hers.

"Ma, I'on know if I even wanna go to college."

Smack!

"What you mean you'on know? Now you listen, and you listen good! You see these hands?" She holds them out palms up. "They are dry and wrinkled and callused from years of hard work. I worked all my life cleaning people houses, rich people. People that had children in college making some'em of themselves. I wanted yo mother to do the same but she got with yo father and he turned her out. When he left her, you wasn't even bon'! And after you was bon' she tried to cope witout'em but it was killin' her to see him wit' another girl, her best friend at that. So she started using the same junk he was sellin' in them streets; it broke my heart to see her sell her body and be used like that, just for a hit or two. So I raised you and I vowed ta neva let that happen to you. I vowed you would go to college and be some'em. So I worked double to pay fo' all them basketball camps, them books and that ballet school you been going to, that stuff sho' ain't free. That was all for this day. Now you sit in my dining room and tell me you don't know if you wanna go ta college? BJ, I will kill you where you sit before I watch these streets take down another one of my blood folks, you hear what I say?"

Bruce takes in every word his grandmother says as he sits at the table. He's still rubbing the warm spot on his face where her right hand connected. Until today, she had never laid a finger on him nor had she ever talked to him with coldness in her voice. It made him realize just how much she's sacrificed for him so that he could have a better life than her and his moms could.

"Ma, I just don't wanna leave you. If something happens to you I'on know what I'll do," he says softly, looking away from her towards the window on his left. "Ma, then there's Ray. I love him like a Brother. I'on wanna leave him behind 'cause he'll never get into any college. He barely made it out of high school."

"That's why you have ta go to college and make a man of yourself. For you first, then me and Ray. Use these hands fo's them basketball courts. Make us proud and get me outta this hell we been living in fo's so long. That's how you give back to me and Ray," she tells him, holding his hands in hers. "Now let's warm this here food up so we can eat." She grabs his plate and walks back to the kitchen. "My little BJ, the NBA superstar."

CHAPTER 6

At one o'clock in the afternoon, the sun is blazing. Kids are in the streets playing in the water which that's shooting from the fire hydrant. Poogie, Shorty, Duce, Big C, and a couple of his boys are sitting on the steps of his building, listening to music and playing bones.

"Sup G? Let me holla at'cha," Ray says as he walks up to Poogie. Poogie gets up immediately and walks over to his boy Ray.

Shorty looks at Big C and asks. "What up wit that nigga? When he start coming on this side of the streets?"

"Got me. Whateva it is, I hope he talks fast 'cause I'm beatin the brakes off Poo's ass!" one of the boys gloats.

"Joe, stop bitchin! I'll jump in and we'll see if you still talking that shit when it's all over," Shorty tells him without taking his eyes off his man, Poogie.

"Sup G?" Poogie greets, giving Ray some thug love hand smack and a shoulder lean.

"You, G. Looka here. I'm tryna get outta this hell hole and I know you are, too. That's always been our dream. You and my brother used ta talk about that shit all the time, right?"

"Right. So what it do?" Poogie asks.

"I came to holla at you 'cause I know you's a real thorough nigga and shit."

"True dat, true dat."

"So I was thinking, I work for old man Rogers spot and I'm thinking I'll keep working fo'em while I get my ski low on. Feel me?" Ray tells him, waiting for his reaction.

"So what you sayin? You tryna sling them bricks?" Poogie comes out and asks with no chasa.

"I'm sayin' let's get this paper. I already hollered at that nigga Youngbleed. Him and my brother go way back and he owes him a favor since he's in the joint holdin' it down fo'em. He said he'll front us five bricks and dat nigga Money said he'll teach me how to cook that shit up so we won't need a middle, feel me?"

"Ok, but why me?" Poogie wonders.

"You know every crackhead in Chi-town. With my connects and your popularity, we can rule this town."

"Let me ask you dis, though: Where do Money come in at'? 'Cause I ain't seen that nigga since I'on know when. Plus, I'on trust his ass. He twitch too fuckin' much."

"He don't come in nowhere. He's out the game as of today. He's moving meth now. He says it's more money but the risk is higher and I'on know 'bout you, but I ain't 'bout that game. Them ABC boys giving out football numbers behind that shit. Feel me?" Ray informs.

"Like a tight rubber."

They both laugh.

"But Ray, man. I think we should keep it soft. That's where the money at these days. If we can get them bricks, I can step on'em a few times and push them joints easy. No cookin' needed. I got a mad ass crew that be pushing that weed for a nigga in Indi but we can drop all that and change the game up," Poogie assures Ray.

Ray rubs his chin hairs and places his arms over his chest as he ponders on it for a minute.

"You think you can pull it off? Five bricks is a lot to start with ... and them Indiana dudes? I'on know, G."

"Nah, nigga, I don't think. *I know.* 'Cause I'm dat nigga believe dat, that's why you came to me. Am I right?" Poogie gets cocky, knowing his skills. "And besides, Chi-town is all 'bout that dope game. Coke game is Indiana's all the way."

Ray steps back and studies Poogie's face.

"A'ight but man, he only giving us two weeks to move'em."

"How much on them joints?" Poogie asks.

"$75,000. That's $15,000 each. We gon make $25,000. Not much, I know for all the risk we takin' but on the next round we can buy our own from'em for the same down low," Ray sings.

"$25 G's, that'a work 'cause we gon stretch that and make a cool $50G's then we can turn that. We ain't gon' pay ourselves shit in the beginning until we make a quick hundred large a piece and that shit gon' be like taking candy from a baby," Poogie brags.

"Bet. I'ma meet you in front of old man Rogers tonight. We'll hold that shit at this spot and trust me, he won't know a thing."

"Sounds good. So how you wanna communicate?" Poogie quizzes.

"The old way. Beepers. And we only call from throw-a-ways. When you page me, put in 626. That's the code to meet up at old man Roger's spot; if you put in 666, then we meet here in the hunnids in front of your building. We'll use this system in the beginning until we come up with another one. And neva, I mean *neva* do we ride dirty or hold. I'll have Youngbleed drop the shit off to me at old man Rogers and you have one of your goons come pick dat shit up. Another thing—no bad whips, no big ass houses on this side of town; if we get jazzy, we gotta do that shit outside of town, another state or place. And keep all niggas outta our business. Now friends, that there will get us dead. We can't get hot, so we gotta lay low. I hope you can respect me on dat shit?" Ray runs it down to him.

"Damn, man, you thought that shit through, didn't you youngster? But all that shit sounds good ta a G like myself. Hell, I've been living low fo' years so that ain't no problem," Poogie explains.

"Bet, let's do this. Let's get this paper," Ray says.

"I'm wit' that." Poogie gives the last word. They dap, half-hug, then Ray walks off and Poogie makes his way back to the porch, thinking how he can cut his main man Shorty Duce in on the deal. But it is what it is. Ray laid the law down and he agreed.

"What's up? What that nigga Ray want?" Shorty Duce puts his nose in.

"Nutten G, just some short talk 'bout old man Roger and shit."

Shorty observes that his man Poogie is lying, but he decides to put it to the back of his mind, feeling if he wanted him to know he would tell him at a later date.

Shorty Duce and Poogie go way back, although Poogie is three years older than him and Ray. Poogie has always looked out for both of them. Poogie loves Shorty Duce like a brother and loves Ray like a brother. He and Ray's brother are very close; they started the weed game together, but when Ray's brother Curt-bone started hanging with Youngbleed, he turned the weed business over to

Poogie and walked away. Two years later, he was popped and took the fall for Youngbleed. Curt-bone is now serving a 15-year sentence, and the only people that take care of him is Poogie and Ray. Youngbleed makes it known to all of his goons that if you get popped, you on your own until the people free you. His standards are like the mobs: you get popped, you take the fall, you stand on your own two. But when you get out, you'll have a party and plenty of money/women to boot.

"So what that old man up to? Carrying his joint like he the real Roy Rogers he's got people going up in there thinking they at Roy Rogers fo' real," Shorty lets out just to see what his boy can come up with.

"Nigga, you got jokes. Nah, that nigga Ray was thinking 'bout buying that joint off'em," Poogie lies once again to his right-hand man.

"Word. So what you say?" Shorty asks.

"I told'em let's look at some numbers."

"Nigga, you'in got no paper like that."

"Nah, but the bank do. It's called a loan," Poogie fires back.

"Loan my ass. Ain't no bank gon' loan shit to no broke-ass black nigga selling weed," Shorty clowns.

Poogie starts thinking, *Which is why Ray said that no one could know, not even your closest, 'cause Shorty just put his business on Front Street and he doesn't even realize it.*

"Joe, shut yo stupid *ignit* ass up and play these bones," one of his boys yells.

They continue to play bones as Poogie thinks of all the money he's getting ready to put down.

"Joe, it's hot," one man shouts, wiping his forehead.

"As hell!" Poogie responds, picking up a cold brew from the cooler.

CHAPTER 7

"Bruce, come get the phone," old man Rogers yells though the kitchen.

"The phone? Joe, take over. Watch my fries," Bruce says to Ray.

"I got that."

Bruce rushes to the back of the kitchen into the office, hoping his grandmother is ok. He takes the phone from old man Rogers. "Hello?"

"Hey son, I need you to come home. It's a man here to see you," his grandmother shouts.

"What man, ma?"

"Just come home, son. It's good news and I already told Mr. Roger to let you come home for a minute. He said you could take the rest of the day off."

"But Ma, I gotta work. I gotta pay my cell phone bill tomorrow and we get paid today."

"Look, I said there's a man here, now come home."

"Ma, is it a college scout? 'Cause—"

"Boy, if you don't get your black ass home," she cuts him short, whispering.

"Ok, joe I'm coming. I'll be there in 30 minutes."

"Thirty minutes, boy? You only five minutes away. Bruce Devon Jones, if you don't hurry yo little ass up ..."

"A'ight, I'll be there in ten minutes. Let me punch out."

"Now that's more like it," she tells him and then hangs up her government phone.

"Sup wit you?" Bruce looks over at Mr. Roger, handing him the receiver.

"Oh nothing, but promise me one thing: when you sign, you'll come back here and visit. We can take some pictures for the restaurant."

"Whateva," Bruce makes an about-face as he starts exiting the office, looking back at old man Roger as if he has two heads because he's still smiling, and Bruce never saw the old man smile before.

Bruce walks out his office wondering who is waiting for him at his crib to make his grandmother call him away from his job.

"Who was that on the phone? Is the old lady ok? I know it had to be important 'cause old man Roger wouldn't have let you take the call," Ray says, never taking his eyes off the burgers he's flipping.

"Yeah man, it was Ma. She said some man waitin' for me at the crib and to hurry home."

"Maybe it's somebody from NCU. They did send you a letter."

"Beats me. But she wants me to come home. He must be important 'cause she called me by my whole government name."

They both look at one another laughing.

"Old man gon' let you go?" Ray needs to know.

"Yeah, that cat was smiling ear-to-ear when I left the office. I think that nigga gon' crazy or some'em," Bruce tells him.

"Look like to me you better get yo punk ass home fo' the old lady come looking fa yo ass," Ray teases.

***

Bruce enters the apartment and sees a young, clean-cut white man sitting in his grandmother's favorite chair that's covered with clear plastic. The man stands, holding his hands out towards Bruce.

"You must be Mr. Jones?"

"Yeah, that's me."

"I'm Arnold Salone. I'm a scout for the Chicago Bulls."

"The what? The who?" Bruce is lost right about now.

Mr. Salone smiles. "The Chicago Bulls. Have a seat," he orders Bruce in his own home.

"Oh. Oh yeah, my bad," Bruce says, then the three of them take a seat. Bruce's grandmother sits next to him and Mr. Salone takes a seat back in the same chair, leaning forward.

"Bruce, I'm going to get straight to the point. Your high school coach sent our organization some clips of your games. And I must say that you're a very good player. I mean, you jump higher than the infamous Michael Jordan. Now that's pretty damn high. Your rebounds are unheard of. I have never seen a player like you. Your grandmother was saying how you took ballet. I guess those lessons paid off, huh?"

"I guess." Bruce hunches his shoulders, still wondering if he's dreaming.

"You guess, you guess?!" His grandmother is overwhelmed. "Bruce, this is a chance of a lifetime. What do you mean, you guess? This man has come all the way here to tell you that his organization—a pro one at that—wants your talent on their team."

Bruce turns his attention back to Mr. Salone, a little agitated with his grandmother. "Excuse her. What are we talking?"

"For starters, a new house in the suburbs and a new Cadillac Escalade truck, along with a four-year, two million dollar contract, and a $100,000 sign-on bonus as our new power forward."

Bruce's grandmother jumps up and does a dance. "Yes, Yes! Thank you Jesus!" she shouts, waving her hands side-to-side in the air.

Bruce looks at her as if she's lost it. "Ma, calm down. I don't even know if I want to take the offer."

"What, boy? You done lost yo eva-lovin' mind!" she snaps, forgetting the scout is still there. "Oh sorry, forgive me," she says and sits back on the sofa, giving Bruce the don't-fuck-this-up look.

"No problem, you have every right to be happy for your grandson. All the hard work you put in paid off. However, your grandson has every right to hold out. He is a very good player."

"No, it's not like that. I just need a day or two to soak it all in," Bruce tells him.

"How about I throw in another $100,000 as a sign-on to shake things up a bit, and make you a final offer of 2.5 million. After all, you are on the top of our organization's list."

"I am?" Bruce is baffled.

"You are. Son, talent like yours doesn't come every day, so when we see it, we do what we can to bring the talent to our team," he informs Bruce.

"Mr. Salone, can you give me a day to get back with you? No disrespect, but I want to talk to my best friend first."

"I understand. I'll give you one week from today. Here is my card." Mr. Salone reaches in his suit jacket, pulls out his card and hands it to Bruce. "Thanks, Mr. Jones. Ms. Smith, you have a good day."

"No, thank you for coming all this way to my home. Do come again," she tells him, smiling.

He turns to Bruce. "Mr. Jones, please remember our organization was the first to come your way."

"I'll keep that in mind. Sir, you have a good day as well." Bruce downplays his excitement. "I'll call you, sir," Bruce says and closes the door behind him. He turns to his grandmother. "Ma, we did the damn thing, didn't we?"

"Yes, we did indeed, but we owe it all to the man upstairs, so don't forget to thank him tonight when you say your prayers."

"No doubt, Ma … no doubt."

CHAPTER 8

Ray's so happy for his boy Bruce. He told him to take the offer. He reminded him how good the Bulls used to be, and that 2.5 million was a lot of loot—even if it was spread out over a four-year period. He told him it was better than going to a four-year college, playing ball and hoping like hell he didn't get hurt before turning pro. Bruce promised Ray that he would take him with him out of the slums, but Ray wasn't having it. This was his life. A real man finds his own way so he turned his offer down, flat. Then, Bruce told him he would make sure Ray always has season tickets to the games and tickets for all of the out-of-town games as well. Then he took him up on it and wished his man the best.

Ray always wanted the best for his friend Bruce. Now that he got what he wanted, he could move on with his life and make a man of himself as well.

Ray walks into Poogie's building on his way home. He knocks on Poogie's apartment door.

"Who dat?"

"Holla at yo boy," Ray yells through the door.

Poogie opens his door and steps outside.

"You get that stuff yo boy picked up?" Ray asks.

"And you know dis. We already broke it down. I got soldiers footin' as we speak."

"That's wussup." Ray is excited but he shows no expression, trying to play boss man. "So you can trust these dudes?" Ray is concerned because he doesn't want to end up like his brother.

"With my life. But no worries. None of them live around here. They some niggas on the Westside of the tracks. So they good."

"OK, but remember Youngbleed wants his return in two weeks."

"G, we gon have dat shit in two days. Stop stressin'."

"Word?"

"Word. My niggas is on it. We using an old, rundown house out in Gangstaville over in Indi as our trap. One of my ex-bitches' moms own that joint. She let it go when her son got smoked in the joint, so it's ours for now. I'll feed her some'em proper-like when we get up."

"Sounds good to me. So I'ma get up wit a nigga, let's say Friday. Ay, let me ask you some'em, it's been botherin' me. No disrespect," Ray fires.

"Shoot," Poogie returns.

"Do Shorty Duce know anything 'bout this business we got goin'?" Ray needs to know.

"Nah, I ain't fuckin' wit'em like that. He runs his gums too much for a nigga," Poogie tells him.

"A'ight, just askin'. So I'll catch you in four."

"Four days it is," Poogie repeats.

They give one another some dap and Ray exits the building. As he walks down the steps, he locks eyes with the sexy Kim. She looks him up and down, undressing him with her eyes, but Ray pays her no mind. She never turned him on, not even in high school. Ray doesn't like Fly girls. He likes natural girls, not doctored up women. Although he thinks Kim is sexy as hell and beautiful, he just feels she's not for him. He nods his head her way and continues to walk.

"Girl, that's Ray. His ass is still fine as fuck! *Woo* child. I remember when he used to play football in school all the girls wanted his ass. I'on know why you ain't neva get'em. Oh, that's right. He used to mess with your arch enemy Shwondia. That country lookin' girl with no ass or tits," Carman says, being funny.

"Yeah, but who cares?" Kim says. "He's nobody anyway. Youngbleed has it all."

"You're right about that, but the magic word is *he* has it all, not you. And as far as I can see, you still in the 'hood. Where is Youngbleed? I'll give it to you; he got you rockin' all the fly shit but you still walking around this ghetto ass hood." Carman hits a nerve.

"Whateva, Carman. And for your 411, I just started fuckin' wit the nigga and he ain't had none yet. Give a bitch time." Carman hit a nerve.

"Bitch, how much time do a rich-ass powerful nigga need? Y'all been kickin' it for six months now. Even if he ain't hit, you still should be driving and livin' in a high-class house somewhere."

"Damn, bitch. Who's countin'?" Kim is pissed.

"I'm not, but you are now, that I am sure of."

"Bitch, I ain't countin' shit."

"No, you not countin' the months on you and Youngbleed, but yo ass is countin' on getting that fine ass Ray, ain't you? You been after that nigga for years now and his ass don't be payin' yo ass no mind."

"Fuck you, bitch! Like you can get'em. As a matter of fact, since you his cheerleader, why you ain't go after his ass?"

"'Cause I'm a real bitch wit' it. He don't want my fat ass and if he did, I would fuck and suck his ass all day and night. His fine coconut ass."

And that she is right about. Ray is a fine brother. His coconut-cream colored brown complexion sets his cold black eyes off. He has curly hair that's always tapered. He has a full beard, mustache, and a goatee that he keeps trimmed close to his face. He's bowlegged, six-foot-three and cut the fuck up with some soft-looking sexy lips. He always smells good and he's always dressed to kill, thanks to his booster.

"If I wanted him I could have him," Kim adds.

"Kim, I love you but sorry boo, 'cause after lookin' at that fine specimen, my kitt kat is purring. So I'll see you when this hot-ass sun goes down. I'm going to call my boo."

Kim continues to stand on the porch, admitting to herself that every time she sees Ray, he rattles her cage. She always wondered why he never paid her any attention. Even though she's with Youngbleed, she still yearns for Ray. She knows Youngbleed has other women and that shit that her homegirl was spitting about not having nothing to show for being with one of the richest men in Chi-town hurts, but it is true. She can't be mad at her for keeping it one hunnid. She goes into deep thought as to how she can get the one man she really wants, even if he is broke.

"Damn, dick on the run is always fun," she says out loud to herself as she turns to go inside.

CHAPTER 9

Ray enters Loretta Penitentiary located in Philadelphia. The C.O.'s check him in and he takes a seat while waiting for his brother Curt-bone to come out.

"Hey man, what up wit' ya?" His brother is so happy to see him.

"Hell, I can't call it. What it be like for you up in this joint?" Ray spits.

"Shit the same damn shit er' day. How is life treatin' my youngsta?"

"G, I'm hanging tryna eat, that's all. That's one of the things I wanted to holla at you about."

"You got my attention," his brother says.

"I'm thinking 'bout working them streets."

His brother sits back in his chair, crossing his arms over his chest. He can't believe his ears, not his little brother.

"I know you'on want me out there like that but I gotta do me. I'm a grown ass man. You know I gotta find my own way." Ray pauses.

"And what way would that be? Slingin' dope fo' another nigga? G, you ain't thinking. Look around you. What do you see?"

"It ain't like dat, man. I'm doing my own thing. I ain't working fo' shit, it's me and Poogie pulling our weight. Dat nigga Youngbleed frontin' us some. We gon pull a quick fiddy off that joint, then we gon' cop our own shit and do the damn thing."

Rays brother is uneasy about the whole thing, but it's one thing that stands true. Ray is his own man and no matter how much Curt-bone tells him not to do it, he's gonna do it. When a nigga is hungry, he'll feed himself—and that there is fa sho real talk.

"Ok, if you do this and if you fuckin' wit that nigga Youngbleed, it's some shit you must know."

"My ears are yours," Ray tells him, chiming in on what his brother is feeding him.

When his brother is finished clueing him in on all he knows, they catch up on life. When the visit is over, Ray promises his brother that he has the true blood of their father. He tells him he will take care of everything, not to worry about nothing.

Ray's brother feels good about what he and Ray talked about. He wishes Ray well and tells him he wants him to come visit him at least once a month. Ray assures him he will, so that's when he makes his exit.

On the way back to the airport, Ray can't help but feel like he let his brother down. He really had no clue as to what was going on, why his brother was really in. All he knew was what the streets was bleeding. He turns his rental in and heads back home.

CHAPTER 10

"G! Y'all hear? That nigga Bruce did it! He made it. He's on the tube. That nigga number one draft pick. He did it!" Shorty Duce yells through the streets, running up to Poogie and his boys that's sittin' on the porch. He's out of breath. He bends over, holding his knees. "G, you hear? That nigga Bruce did it. He made the Bulls. G, he's gon be representin' the Hunnids," he continues to brag.

"I know. We heard."

"What? How y'all bitch as niggas know before me?"

"'Cause Big Ed told us this morning," Poogie informs him.

"How he know? It just came over the waves and shit?" Shorty Duce asks with his top lip turned up and one hand resting on his hip.

"Don't know, but he already told us this morning. You playin' bones or you gon ride that niggas dick all day?" Poogie asks.

"Nah, I'm good. I'ma holla at you later."

"Ay G, c'mon it ain't even like dat." Poogie walks off the porch, seeing as though his man is fucked up because he didn't let him in on the fact that one of their 'hood stars made a come up.

Shorty Duce turns around and faces his boy Poogie. "Naw nigga, it's just like dat."

"*Aww*... look at the baby boy. Ol' bitch ass nigga," one of the other boys seated on the steps clowns.

"Fuck you! Bring yo ass, I'll show you a bitch," Shorty invites. Poogie holds Shorty back.

"G, what up wit dat? You know that nigga was just clownin'. What up wit' you?" Poogie gets serious with him.

"You, G. I know you rollin'. Talkin 'bout some Rogers sellin' his joint. Nigga, I know you. I know when you lyin'. What that be like? I'm supposed to be yo main man. Your boy and shit."

"First off, I'on know what you talkin' bout and if what you spittin' was true, I'm my own man. G, I got mad love fo' ya but certain lines a real nigga don't cross, and dis here is one of 'em. On the real, you actin' like a bitch. You see me er' day, same place doin' the same shit. Nutten new, then you come on my porch in my 'hood screamin' on a nigga. So who's rollin?" Poogie tries to convince him.

But Shorty Duce is not buying it one bit, and him having a loud mouth just went over his head. He doesn't even get what Poogie is saying. All he knows is that right now he's in his feelings.

"Whateva G, you right nucca, do you." As Shorty Duce allows those words to fly off his tongue, Kim walks across the street.

"Hey, Poo. What's up?" she greets.

"I can't call it," Poogie says, stepping back scanning her sexiness.

"I can," she tells him, looking him up and down with lust in her eyes, but the real of it is that she's smelling money. There is no man in the 'hood holding that makes it past her. It's as if she has a built-in money radar. "So I guess you heard about BJ. He made it to the pros." Kim thinks she's silk, she just wants to confirm the word on the street thinking she may get in with the crew.

"That's what the streets hollerin," he tells her.

"So y'all giving him a party or some'em?" she asks. Kim looks over her shoulder 'cause she feels someone breathing on her. When she sees its Shorty Duce, she turns her lip up. "Why you all up on me like dat? On the real, you'on know me G."

Shorty Duce plays it cool by smirking and stepping back. "My bad."

"My bad too. Did I interrupt some'em?" She turns back to Poogie and asks.

"Nah, not really. We was just shootin' 'hood shit."

"Well, I'll let you finish talking," she tells him.

"A'ight."

Kim makes an about face to walk back across the street. Then she stops in her tracks and looks back at Poogie who's still lusting.

"Poo?" she calls out. "Can I come? I mean to the spot if y'all throw him a party?"

Poogie is lost for words. He doesn't know what to think. Is it a set up or do she like him? In any case, "And you know you can, ma," he spits.

"Good, let me know. See you, Shorty Duce." She smiles and waves at him. He nods his head, still embarrassed.

Round one, Ray, Kim thinks to herself. *You'll be mines before the month is out. Who can resist this $50,000 body? I miss Black's ass so much. He was trickin' a bitch off. May he rest in peace. Ray, I know y'all niggas gettin' it and I need to get in where I fit in.*

"What was dat all about? That bitch ain't neva said two good words to you or any of us," Shorty Duce reminds Poogie, forgetting about the beef he has with him.

"Got me, G," Poogie says, turning to go back on the porch.

"If you ask me, I think she wants you."

"Naw, she's Youngbleed's girl."

"And you say that to say what?" one of their boys named Big C asks.

"G, I'on get down like dat. Now let's take these drinks to the head and hit them bones 'cause dis convo is a wrap," he tells them, pulling the game of dominos out.

CHAPTER 11

One Month Later

Big C, Shorty Duce, Poogie, Ray, and Bruce are seated in the makeshift VIP section of a well-known strip club called The Factory. Ray and Poogie order rounds of drinks and some bottles. Shorty Duce makes a mental of his boy spending paper like its nothin'. They're having the time of their lives. All the strippers come over to see what they're working with. They give them private dances and conversation. Bruce is loving the whole scene.

"G, this is what I call the good life. You told me you was saving money but I had no idea you was saving all of it," Bruce says to his boy Ray.

"Yeah, that's what I do. But this is your day and the sky's the limits."

One of the dancers gives Bruce a lap dance, while the guys make it rain all over her and yelling, "Get 'em, put it on 'em baby!" The dancer goes as far as putting her mouth on the bulge of his pants. Bruce jumps. "Whew, damn ma that feels good!" He's so excited he's about to nut in his pants. His leg is shaking and his eyes widen. He's moving his hips to the movement of her lips. She blows hot air out of her mouth onto the bulge. This drives Bruce crazy. "Ohhhh shit!" he yells over the music.

"Nigga, you a'ight? It's just a lap kiss," Ray laughs.

Bruce is so embarrassed so he plays it off.

"Um, I'm good you know, I just didn't expect all that. That's all." He looks at his man wide eyed. His leg is still shaking.

"Did you nut?" the dancer asks.

"Me?! Who me?"

"Nah, nigga you," she spits, looking him up and down as she remains on her knees.

"No, I didn't nut, what you talkin' bout' did I nut? You funny." He gives a dry laugh, looking over at his boys who are staring at him.

"Then why your pants wet?" she persists.

"That, that's that Hen dog," he lies.

"G, don't tell me you a 19-year-old virgin," Poogie clowns.

"Go ahead man with that shit. It's his night. Let that man have his fun," Ray steps in for his boy. "Excuse me young lady," Ray says to the dancer, putting three dead presidents in her garter. Then he whispers in Bruce's ear as the young lady steps off, "G, you a superstar now, get used to that shit. These hoes gon' be all over you for the rest of your life. See, first you get the money, then the power, then the bitches—in that order. Always play it cool. Never let the next nigga or bitch see your play card."

"I hear what you saying and thanks, G, for er'thing. I mean that," Bruce says with watery eyes.

Shorty sits and watches, taking it all in. He's loving all the girls that are surrounding them. He leans over and whispers in Poogie's ear, "Yo, G, where y'all gettin all this chedda from?"

Poogie's face shows disgust.

"Why you askin', G? Just enjoy the night. Ray's right hand man just went pro, that's all. Ray treatin' us to a good night, nothing more, nothing less. Now stop riding me 'bout my loot." Poogie is getting irritated with him. "I'm startin' ta think yo ass is five-O."

"Neva dat. I was just wondering."

"See that there is the problem, 'cause nobody payin' yo ass to wonder. Now drink up and shut up."

Shorty turns his attention back on the young freak that's bouncing to the music on his hard dick when Kim walks up. Shorty Duce stands up so fast he knocks the girl off his lap. You would have thought Kim was his wife or something.

"Oh shit, my bad baby!" he says, reaching down to help her to her feet.

"What was that all about?" the dancer huffs.

"Here, sit right here," he orders her, pointing to the seat beside him. She follows his orders well.

"Hey y'all," Kim greets.

"Hey, baby girl," Poogie chimes in.

"Who's your friends?" Poogie asks Kim.

"My bad. This is Angie and this is Bey, my partners in crime."

"Well, I would love to take a bite out of crime," Shorty says, looking over at Bey. She smiles, showing the diamond stud in her front tooth.

Ray is scoping Angie out. He looks her up and down. She is not his normal type, but something about her turns him on. She's dark skinned, no breasts, long dreads, but she has a phat ass, and a flat stomach with a six-pack to match. The thing that is turning him on is her unusual eye color. They are a dark grey. He is trying to see if they are contacts when he notices her looking back at him smiling. Her deep dimples sealed the deal.

"Angie, you want something to drink?" Ray asks.

"So is she the only one that gets to drink?" Kim butts in.

He acts as if he doesn't hear Kim, then Poogie invites Kim and Bey to sit and drink.

"I don't drink but I'll have an orange juice," Angie tells him.

This bitch gets on my nerves, Kim thinks to herself. And why he ain't ask me if I wanted some'em to drink. He sittin' over there like he don't see my fine ass. It's ok, 'cause I schooled that hoe before we got here. I told her that Ray was out of bounds. So he won't get none of that ass ta-night.

Angie and Ray talk and dance all night. He's really digging her. Kim is getting pissed and madder by the minute.

"I'ma kick that bitch in her throat. I warned that hoe," she says to Bey. But Bey is so into Shorty Duce's rap game that she's not paying Kim no mind.

"That's my song. C'mon, Ray, let's dance," Kim says, jumping up.

Ray doesn't really want to dance but he gets up and follows Kim to the dance floor. She winds up on him as if he is her man. She even kisses him on his neck. The club is a strip club, but for tonight, they allow Ray and his boys to have their way. Ray dropped some green stacks in the club owner's palm beforehand.

"What is that smell?" Kim asks him with her nose buried in his neck. "I like it."

"Versace."

"Versace, huh?"

"Yep, that's what I said." He is getting irritated. He wants to get back to Angie, who he see's talking to Big C, which he doesn't like.

"Look Kim, I hate to break this little dance up but I gotta get back to the table, plus this don't feel right. You're my man's girl."

"Yo man? Who's your man?"

"Youngbleed."

"When he become yo man?"

"Don't madda. You're his woman and he's my man and that's the end of the convo," he tells her, breaking their embrace and making his way back to the VIP.

This turns her on even more.

"For the record, I'm not his woman. We are just friends!" she yells over the music, walking on Ray's heels.

"Yeah, that's what they all say," he lets out in a low voice, taking his seat next to Angie.

His ass didn't even get hard. Kim is so mad that she goes to the restroom. When she enters, she hears moaning coming from one of the stalls and that makes her even madder, so she goes into a stall and beats her clit off.

CHAPTER 12

Six Months Later

Bruce moved him and his grandmother out of the Hunnids, thanks to the Bulls organization. They purchased them a $700,000 house in the suburbs of Memphis. Bruce's grandmother couldn't be happier to get out of Chi-Town. She's lived there all of her life. She felt a change was good. Bruce didn't want to really leave his town, but he wanted to pay her back for all the years she was there for him. She thanks God everyday as she shops and plays bridge on the weekend with her new rich friends.

Bruce and Ray don't see much of one another since Bruce moved, nor did Bruce keep his promise to Ray about the out of town tickets to see his team play. But he did get him season tickets for the home games, sky box seats. Ray has never missed a home game yet. After all the games, he and Angie always head home to his new house located in Oak Brook, Illinois. It's a hell of a drive, but his man is worth it. Even though they don't talk as they used to, Ray's not mad at him because he's doing him—and as a man, he can't do nothing but respect that.

Ray and Poogie have climbed the ladder. So far, Ray's banked a cool $300G's and Poogie the same. They both have nice houses and nice whips. Poogie is staying in Indiana, one hour away from all the traps. He keeps a close eye on the money along wit' the crew, making sure everything is everything. They go into Chi-Town a lot. They've never given up their 'hood apartments in the Wild Hunnids. They both sport hoopties because they don't want all eyes on 'em. When they go to Chi-Town, they keep a low profile. No iced-out jewelry or fresh gear. Just the same ole 'hood gear and the same attitude they always had. They're keeping things simple. They feel like this will keep the haters at bay.

Angie and Ray are doing their thing. Angie has planned a surprise birthday party for Ray. She has become head-over-heels about her new man. She keeps their life private. He hasn't met her family nor has she met his, even though he has told them about her. Angie has not uttered a word about their relationship, not even to Kim. She knows how Kim feels about Ray so she finds it best to just let that subject be. Angie often wonders how Ray can afford such a lovely house, but she just keeps her mouth shut and enjoys the ride.

Bey has been screwing Shorty Duce, who is now a proud owner of one of the fastest growing dry-cleaning businesses in Chi-Town. It's bringing him in a mint. Poogie bought it for him to keep him off his back. Poogie told him he got a loan for the places. "Don't ask me no questions about it."

Kim and Youngbleed are still kickin' it, but she's still in the 'hood. The one thing that's changed in her life is her new transportation. He bought her a 4-Series BMW. She's happy for now. Even though the 'hood is talking about how she has a car that cost more than where she lays her head. Kim still keeps it moving, not caring about what people got to say about her. Her motto is, "Don't hate the playa. Get with the playa and learn the game."

Carman is doing Carman. She has a new hook up in the game but she keeps it one hunnid. She keeps to herself and she keeps her mouth shut.

CHAPTER 13

"Carman, this shit is gettin' outta hand. Er' time I look around it's more and more shit. I mean now we gotta bury Lil Perry from 'round the way. Who would kill that nigga? He didn't do nutten but go to school and have like a thousand babies by that girl. And whoever the grimy ass nigga was, raped and killed his baby momma too. Now dat there is some fucked up shit!" Ray voices while counting money at Carman's table in her living room.

"I'm with you. But what really gets me is the bitches who don't mind their business. Like Kim, she's always worried about what I'm doing, how I get this and that," she says, getting off the subject. Ray looks at her like she's Frosty the Snowman.

"Carman, what the fuck that got to do with lil man dying? But since you on that subject, if y'all women stop throwing shit up in each other's faces then y'all wouldn't be having them problems. Real talk."

"Maybe you right," she voices, walking to the kitchen then returning with a glass of Kool-Aid in hand, standing over Ray as he deposits more money into the counting machine.

"You know, word is you gunning people down in front of their kids," she spits as she takes a sip of Kool-Aid.

Ray keeps counting. "People will say anything, Carman, you know how that shit goes in these streets."

"Yeah but—"

He stops counting, cutting her off. "Look, Carm. Let me deal wit' the street business and you deal wit' the back end of shit. Now did you do what I asked you to do this morning?"

She sucks her teeth. "Yeah."

"Good, now c'mon let's get down wit' this. Then you can take care of big Daddy," he tells her, smiling.

She does what she's told. Carman and Ray have been getting down since high school. She's always been his sidekick. She knows it's because she's 300 pounds. He never told anyone nor has he ever taken her anywhere. Since his comeup he gives her anything she wants, but to him she is just a piece of hot pie.

What she doesn't know is Ray trusts her before any nigga, just the fact she never told anyone about them—even now that he's with Angie, Carman still keeps her mouth shut. When the going gets tough she never left his side. This why she's still around while the sun is shining.

CHAPTER 14

Poogie sits on his porch well after midnight, chewing on a straw with a cup of Henny in his hand. He's waiting for Ray to pass so they can talk. He got some disturbing news that he needs to put in Ray's ear. Kim spots him as she comes out of her building, walking across the street, looking fine and fresh as always.

"Hey Poo, what you doin' out here without yo boys?"

"Nutten, just coolin'. What up witcha?"

"Same old shit, different damn day. I was getting ready to go get some chow. I was thinking Taco Bell."

"Taco Bell? Baby, it's two in the AM. You might wanna try Mr. Rogers. They open 24-7 now," he informs.

"Oh yeah, that's right. I forgot."

"What you doing eatin' dat junk food anyway?" he asks, observing her body.

"It's betta than nothing. Plus it's late and I'on feel like cookin' shit." She moves closer to him. She's so close that Poogie can feel the beat of her heart. "Can I have some of that in your hand?" she asks in a seductive tone.

He holds up the tall cup in front of her face. "It could be shit in this cup for all you know."

"Don't look like shit to me, but that's not what I want anyway," she states, eyeballing his dick through his shorts. She presses her palms against the bulge in his pants, looking into his eyes. "Do you think you can handle?"

"I know I can handle," he tells her, licking his full lips.

This muthafucka is hung, she's thinking. She follows him in his apartment.

Without saying a word, she takes a hold of his dick in her right hand, bends over, and places the head of it in her mouth. Then she sucks it inside of her jaws. She begins to bobble her head up and down, round and round, with her eyes closed. Kim is enjoying the juicy meat that's between her tight lips.

With her free hand, she unbuttons her top to let her triple F twins in on the fun.

She falls to her knees.

He slides his dick back and forth between her breasts as she continues to suck the life out of his dick. She grabs hold of his balls, massaging them round and round. Then she t-bags them. This makes his dick hard as a bone. It's as hard as his dick has ever been. He looks down at her.

"You gon' give a nigga some of that good-good?" he whispers.

She nods yes, and then bends over in the old famous doggie style position. He drops to his knees, places a raincoat over his dick, spits on her asshole, and starts working his way in.

"Oh shit!" she yells, then jumps a foot out.

"C'mon, ma. Where you goin'? Relax." He's not pleased because she can't seem to handle him.

Resuming her position, he places the head of his dick on the tip of her asshole and pushes it in slowly, each inch further and further.

"*Siss, siss,* shit oh my God, *whew!*" she moans in pain.

"You want a nigga to stop?" he mumbles, hoping she would say no.

"No, it feels so good," she lies.

Once his dick is in, he starts moving slowly, grinding and grinding inside her deep dark tunnel.

"Damn, Kim! This some tight shit, you squeezing the shit outta my Johnson. You ain't never had no dick in yo ass befo', have you?"

She shakes her head no. He smiles because that answer is turning him on even more, knowing he's the first. He thought she was a jump-off, but maybe not.

He places his hand on her shoulders and starts grinding deeper, picking up the pace.

"*Ohhhh! Ahahagh! Shit!*" she yells from the pain she's feeling. But after a while, she starts to relax as she catches his rhythm.

"Relax," he repeats as he starts to pick up speed. He strokes and strokes faster and harder. Her head is moving back and forth. Her body is jerking and her breasts are jumping from the thrusting he's putting on her.

"Yes, *my God,* yes. Get it, *oooh, yes!*" she now yells as her ass loosens up.

"You like dis' dick, don't you bitch? Don't you?" he yells, feeling the pleasures of her treasure.

"Yes, Poo, yes. Don't stop, *pleazzz* don't stop!" she begs as she feels his balls smacking against the back of her pussy. He pulls his dick out of her ass and quickly rips a hole in the condom. The old teenage trick. He wants to feel her raw. He hurries and puts it back so he won't ruin the moment.

"Yes, yes, oh yes, fuck me! *Pleazzz* fuck dis! Fuck me!"

He pushes and pumps, winding, grabbing all her meat. He feels the warmth of her inner walls. He feels his balls swell. He knows it's time.

"*Uh, uh um ahum,*" he grunts.

"Cum, cum nigga, cum!" she huffs, throwing her ass back harder.

"*Ahhhhh!* SHIT BITCH, SHIT!" he yells, grabbing her hair, pulling it back as he busts nut up in her.

He slows down, biting her on her back, leaving a trail of passion. When he pulls out, she turns around to take another look at his big dick. She's never seen a dick so big.

"Boy, the condom broke."

"I know, you good? 'Cause I know I'm good," he tells her with a straight face.

"Yeah, but I ain't on the pill."

"Well if I made a bun tonight, then you will have to decide to have it or get rid of it. Plus, I was only in your pussy for like five minutes. I nutted in that ass."

She smiles. "Poo, you funny."

After laying his dick game down on her, Kim now looks at him in a different light.

Poogie is not a looker. He puts you in the mind of the rapper Jay Z. He dresses good and he keeps himself well groomed, but he is not Ray. It's one thing that turns bitches on about Poogie: he's got swagga, and nobody questions his gangsta, not even Youngbleed, one of the toughest muthafuckas in the 'hood. Ray and Poogie are good with their hands and quick to make peace. That's the life they choose. That's the only life they know, 'hood fears them.

"So when can a nigga hit again?" he boldly says.

She looks at him and smiles. "Tomorrow."

"Tomorrow? Negative, how about in a few."

"Ok," she tells him, looking shy. She gets dressed, kisses him on his cheek and heads for the door. Before she could get out ...

"As a matter of fact, be back in my presence at 12 noon," he tells her.

"Whateva."

As she walks out of the building door, she bumps into Ray.

"Excuse you!" she greets with attitude, feeling herself now that she's in with the crew.

Ray smirks and walks around her as if she wasn't even standing in front of him.

Kim starts to feel a rush of guilt because it's Ray that she really wants, but she knows she can't have him.

CHAPTER 15

It's five in the morning and the sun is starting to rise. Poogie and Ray pull up to the Gangstaville Trap. They park across the street so no one will see them. The two of them use their key to gain entry. When they walk in, they see that the house is a mess.

"Where's Pee and Pinky?" Poogie asks as he taps Cockeye on the bottom of his feet. The brotha is laying across the dirty sofa in a deep sleep.

"Huh, what?" Cockeye says, rubbing his eyes yawning.

"Nigga, get yo ass up! I say where Pee and Pinky?" Poogie asks again as Ray stands back and observes. He is thinking, *Why is this nigga repeatin' himself?*

"Oh um, they in the back."

"C'mon, then let's go. We having a family meetin'," Poogie utters.

They all gather in the dining room. Some are standing and some take a seat.

"Rest yo backs gentlemen," Ray gives a command.

"Who you?" Pee huffs.

"Don't madda. I said rest yo fuckin' back," Ray says again, taking one step closer to Pee, who is only standing a foot away.

"Who dis nigga coming up in here givin' orders?" Pee looks at Poogie questioning Ray's gangsta.

Ray looks at Poogie. "You'on gotta answer to shit this punk-ass nigga askin'." Then Ray looks at Pee again, then at the other two men that are still standing. "I'm not gon' tell y'all again. I don't make a habit of repeatin' my words," Ray states, pulling back his jacket, showing off his Glock .40 with its pearl-white handle. He had it specially made, and it's a beauty.

"Just sit down, man," Twin whispers, looking up at his brothers, Pee and Pinky, who don't seem to wanna take orders from the man they've never laid eyes on.

They look at one another, then at Poogie who nods his head in agreement, then they finally join the rest of the men.

"Good, now let's get down to business. My man Poo tells me we havin' some technical difficulties."

"What?" Pee curves his upper lip and raises his eyebrow, gangsta-ing up.

"Nigga, did I ask you to speak?"

Bloc! Bloc! is the sound that rings in all their ears. Poogie can't believe Ray just peeled back Pee's wig within a split second. None of them saw the two shots to his head Ray just delivered coming. Blood splattered all over the table and on some of the other men, but they say nothing. They don't make a move. They just tremble and wait for orders. Without flinching or looking Pee's way again, Ray continues to talk, lowering his hammer to his side.

"I'ma try dis shit one mo' again. Me and my man here …" Ray waves his .40 from his body to his boy Poogie. "… We coming up short on our dead backs, like 10G's short. Would any of you fellas happen to know where we can find that shit?"

Ray stands, waiting for someone to speak up, crossing his hands over his chest still holding his Glock. Twin raises his hand.

"Speak," Ray orders.

Twin looks over at Pinky. Pinky looks at Cockeye and Don looks at Moe. While Twins brother nods his head, as if to say, "No, don't do it."

"So ain't nobody talking. None of y'all niggas know shit?" Ray quizzes as he gets madder and madder by the second.

"It was Don," Twin blurts out faster than lightening could strike.

"YOU SNITCH ASS NIGGA!" Don hollers.

Bloc! Bloc!

81

Before Don could finish his sentence, Ray sends him to meet Jesus.

"Now if we miss one dime next week, the FBI gon' be drawing chalk around all y'all bitch-ass niggas. Clean these niggas up. C'mon, Poo. Let's ride."

Poogie follows behind Ray in shock. Not because he shot his boys. He's seen Ray kill many times before, but he is shocked that he's leaving witnesses. All the men release their breath, relieved they didn't lose their life today, but to their dismay and to Poogie it comes as no surprise when Ray turns back around.

Bloc! Bloc! Bloc! Bloc! Bloc!

Poogie jumps as Ray kills everything moving. Ray then looks over at Poogie. "I thought you said you trust them wit' yo life?"

"I thought I could."

"Well, man, it looks like Ray and Poogie enterprises is hiring. I'ma get the chainsaw. We got a lot of work ahead of us this morning," Ray tells him.

"Nah, man, let's just torch this bitch, it's enough empty houses around here to move our action to."

"That sounds like a plan," Ray says.

They pull the gas can from the closet and pour it throughout the abandoned house. Cockeye moves. He is still breathing. He lifts his head as Poogie throws gas on his face.

"I'm alive. Help!" he musters up.

Poogie sees that he is alive. He hears him, but he lights the gas bomb he made and throws it anyway. Then they run out the door.

BOOM! is the next sound they hear as they walk to the car. They get in, looking on as the flames burn high.

"Let's ride," Ray tells Poogie. They ride all the way home, making small talk as the sounds of The Migos bounce through the speakers.

CHAPTER 16

It's eleven at night. Angie and Ray are getting dressed at his house in Oak Brook, Illinois.

"Bae, I still think it's sad what happened in Indi. Them people in that abandoned house. The saddest thing is they still didn't catch the people that did it," Angie voices while standing at the dresser, looking in the mirror, applying her eyeliner, while Ray sits on the end of his bed, putting on his shoes.

"Yeah, babe, that was pretty fucked up but you know how it goes. They was black and probably in the dope game so ... them pigs just step back and watch us kill one another, know'imean?"

"I know, but they had a mother, a father, sister, brother and maybe a child. Whoeva did that to 'em ... I hope they rot in hell!"

"C'mon, bae, you'on know what them niggas was into, and fa' real, it could have just been an accident or a real fire," he tells her, not really caring.

"The news said it was set by gasoline and the bones of the remains had bulletholes in'em. Who could be so cold?" she turns to him and asks, then makes a turnabout facing the mirror. "I'm just glad you didn't follow that path."

Ray walks up behind her, grabbing her around the waist.

"Let's not think about that 'cause tonight is my night. Yo man's birthday. All we need to do is meet Poo and the boys at the club and enjoy ourselves."

She smiles as he kisses her nape. When they finish getting ready, they head out the door.

Buzz ... *buzz* is the vibration of Angie's phone she holds in her hand. She glances over at Ray with a sneaky look about her, then at her caller ID.

"You gon' answer it?" he looks over her shoulder and asks.

"Naw, that's Kim. And she'on won't shit but gossip," she lies.

"Y'all girls are crazy as hell," he says, holding the car door open for his woman.

***

One hour later, they enter the parking lot of The Factory Strip Club.

"Bae, where er'body at? Is dis joint closed?" he asks.

"I don't think so."

"Let me call Poo and make sho dis the right joint. I could've sworn he said The Factory."

"It's some cars out here. I mean maybe the club ain't packed yet," she says with her hand on the door handle. She turns to him. "Bae, you actin' like you a big time dope boy or some'em. Don't worry, ain't nobody gon' hurt a saleswoman and her man," she teases.

He looks over at her. *If only you knew*, he thinks to himself.

"C'mon, let's go." She rushes out the car, slamming the door making her way to the club.

"Hold on, Angie, let me call Poo," he yells out the car window.

"Boy, c'mon," she tells him, walking toward the club leaving him behind.

Ray hurries out his car and catches up with her. They walk to the club. Ray is scanning the parking lot, making sure it's not a setup. They open the doors to the club. Ray notices there isn't a sound. No music, no cashier, no bouncer. It's kinda dark as well.

"Angie, bae let's go!" he lets out, grabbing her by the arm.

"SURPRISE!" His boys jump out from everywhere.

"Ay ... man! Y'all niggas got me fa' real!" Ray laughs, giving them all gangsta leans.

Ray steps back, looks at his boy Poogie. He opens his arms, signaling his man to show some brotherly love.

"Nigga, what I look like, yo bitch?" Poogie shoots, laughing.

"Never dat," Ray answers.

"Yeah, I saw you watching the parkin' lot like a hawk." Poogie laughs, then Ray looks over at Angie. "You knew?" Angie nods her head yes, smiling. "C'mere girl." He grabs her around her neck.

Bruce walks up to him, which makes Ray feel good knowing his main man is showing him lots of love. "Angie did a good job planning this party. She hired The Migos, Jeremiah, K. Michelle, and Rick Ross to perform. She even asked Stevie J and Joseline to come through."

"Word?" Ray says, looking Angie up and down. "That's how my boo doin' it, huh?"

"And you know this," she says jokingly.

They all go into the club. The house is packed by the time of the show, with people Ray knows and doesn't know. All courtesy of Poogie, who footed the bill.

It's the end of the night. All the programmers did their thing and everyone had a good time. Ray has a dancer on his lap and the real ballers are making it rain. Then Angie stands on the stage with a mic in her hand. Her voice is heard throughout the club.

"Hello everyone. Can I get yall's attention?" She now owns the crowd's eyes and ears. The DJ stops the music. "I just wanna say thanks to all y'all for making my man's night so special." She turns her attention to the performers. "Thanks for coming. I know y'all could have been other places, but y'all came out. Thanks again. Damn good show!" They nod their heads and hold up their drinks as they sit at the table. Then she gives her attention to Bruce, who is standing on the right of Ray and Poogie. "Bruce, thank you so much. Without you, this couldn't have been. You're a great friend, a wonderful person to know. I want you to know that I'm your biggest fan, and wit' that said let's toast to you and Ray."

The crowd holds up their drink of choice in their glasses. Poogie's face is a dead giveaway of pissed off because he paid for the whole thing. He gave Bruce the money to give to Angie, but he couldn't let her know he paid for it all. Ray takes notice of his man's face, but he decides to wait until the party is over before asking him what was up.

K. Michelle takes the stage to sing happy birthday to Ray. He licks his chops.

"*Damn now that there is a FATT ASS!*" Then he looks at Angie, who is seated beside him. "But I got you. Bae, this is the best birthday party a nigga has ever had. Well, it's the only birthday party I've eva had." Good save on his part.

"Not bad for a high scale computer saleswoman, huh?" she jokes.

"Not bad at all," he repeats, wishing he could tell her he's a millionaire for real.

He excuses himself and mingles with his guests.

"Hey, Big C baby, *ba-by.*" They give one another a gangsta lean. "Who dat?" Ray asks.

"Oh, her? Just a jump off," Big C tells him, looking over at his date. She smiles.

"G, why you always gettin' them girls with no teeth?"

"Ray man, that's how I like 'em. See, I wait outside the dentist office and the one that comes out wit' no teeth ... I be like, girl, come to poppa. I got a hard teeth ring for you and you'on even gotta put it in the freezer."

Ray and the other boys burst into hard laughter.

"Man, you got unresolved issues," Ray tells him, and then makes his way to Bruce.

"What you laughing at?" Bruce asks.

"Nutten man, that nigga C is off the fuckin' chain."

"You'on know?"

"So what up, G? I see yo year was like a *fiah* cracker. Thirty-five points a game ... damn, you killin'em and them assists per fuckin' game, boy you doin' some big things. They gon' renew that contract yet." Ray's so happy for'em.

"You saw me on the tube, huh?" Bruce fishes.

"The tube?! Hell nah, I be at er' game. I'on miss none of 'em."

Bruce looks at him, leaning back with his drink in hand. "Why you'on come holla at me after the games? I got you backstage passes!"

"I'm good. I know you my man. I show my love by being at the game. No need for me coming up in the joint looking like one of your fans and shit. I'll leave that to the ladies. Did you have fun watching the show, 'cause I know you paid a grip for it."

"Nah, it wasn't me. It was Poo. Man, he put the damn thing down. All I did was hand the green backs to yo girl. Speakin' of which, I see y'all gettin hot and heavy."

"Some'em like dat," Ray utters.

"Do I hear wedding bells?" Bruce teases.

Ray looks at him holding his drink. "Do you think she's wifey material?" He takes a swallow.

"As long as I'm the best man."

"That you and Poo gon' haveta fight for," Ray tells him, kind of in his feelings about Bruce not chipping in for his birthday.

Bruce quickly changes the subject. "Look, man, I got some'em fo' ya." Bruce pulls an envelope from his pocket, handing it to Ray. Ray looks at it. "Open it," Bruce orders.

Ray tears it open, pulling out a check that reads $50,000 large.

"You shouldn't have." Ray flashes a fake smile.

"I did. I know you could use the money. Take yo bun out and get her some'em nice. I know you got your own thing goin' with Mr. Rogers, but this is for you. Put some'em down on a fuckin' car and get rid of that hooptie." Bruce is so proud of his gift. If only he knew what he just gave Ray is small beans. He makes that in one hour or less, but it helps remind Ray he's doing a good job of covering his tracks.

Angie walks over and Bruce's eyes light up. Ray takes notice as he feels his man is undressing his woman. He feels some kind of way about the both of them. The toast she gave. It's not adding up in his mind, but he dismisses it as an act of being kind. When it's all said and done, Ray thanks everyone as they exit the club. He goes backstage to meet the hired superstars of the night. When they're gone, he and Poo make their exit.

"Holla at me in the morning, say 11 o'clock. We got some shit to talk about." Poogie embraces his man and laces his ear with a little news he found out.

"I'll be there," Ray assures. "Oh, I almost forgot." Ray gives his man some dap and a half shoulder tap, then he looks him in his eyes. "Man, I know you gave Bruce the money. Thanks so much."

Poogie feels better now that he knows who really paid for his bash. "Fa' sho', you know you my main man."

"I'll see you in the morning," Ray tells him and he's ghost.

CHAPTER 17

Ray and Angie make it back to his house. "Why you don't never park in the garage?" she asks.

"I got mad shit in dat joint. Why?" He keeps the door locked to the garage because he doesn't want her to see all his cars.

"But it's like a ten-car garage," she adds.

He turns to her, still sitting behind the steering wheel of his hooptie. "Bae, why you hounding me about my garage? Are you five-O or some'em?"

"Hell no! I was just wondering when you was gon' buy a car to park in the bitch." She's in her feelings now.

"One day. I'm *part* owner of Rogers, not the owner," he reminds her.

"You got it. I won't ask ever again," she tells him, stepping out his Honda Accord.

They walk up the wide stairway and enter his master bedroom. Angie grabs her overnight bag.

"I'ma go freshen up a bit."

"Ok," he tells her, thinking that she's going to do her usual and blow him off.

When Angie returns, she stands in the well-lit doorway of his room. She allows her wrap to drop to the marble floor, revealing that she's wearing nothing but a sheer linen gown. Ray's dark eyes look her body up and down, for he can now clearly see much more than the outline of Angie's small breasts and the sway of her lovely hips. The heat between the two isn't one-sided. Angie knows all too well the power of seduction and she is about to bestow upon Ray her most precious treasure.

He moves close to her, placing his manly hands on her face, as he looks her in those innocent beautiful gray eyes. She blinks, pressing her lips against his. Their tongues do a love dance. Angie feels a rush of heat flow through her body. He lifts her up. She wraps her long slender legs around his waist.

Ray pulls her hair back, exposing the veins of her neck. He sinks his teeth in, biting down aggressively over and over.

Angie's pussy becomes overly moist. She's never felt this way with any other man. She wants Ray to fulfill her every craving. She leans back in his arms as he bites through her gown, sucking and biting on her tender dark nipples. "*Siss*, oh yes!" she hisses as she holds on to his neck with her eyes closed. Ray drops his boxers to the floor. His dick is full of hot blood. With one swift movement, he places both hands on her butt cheeks ... then he inserts his penis in the wet ocean that awaits him.

Blood starts to escape her opening.

"*Awwww! Awww!*" she whispers, biting down on her bottom lip. The pain of passion is excruciating. She continues to moan with every thrust he delivers. Ray walks her over to his round waterbed. He gently lays her down on her back, never allowing his manhood to fall out. He's pushing up in her further. She feels as though he's penetrating her soul. A tear cascades down her face. She quivers as he makes true love to her, kissing and grinding, kissing, and grinding.

"Ray, *pleazzz Ray,* I love you so much. Don't let this end, *pleazzz!*" She hums.

She isn't alone. Ray feels the passion as well. *This is the best pussy in my life. I love you so much too, girl,* his mind plays over and over, as he continues to administer the best love-making session ever. He pulls his dick to the surface of her pussy. The head of his dick slowly pierces in and out of her wet opening.

"Ray, My God! Ray, *pleazzz!*"

Her legs shiver as thick white juices flow down Ray's dick. Ray presses forward, filling her inner womb, then he exits rapidly. Her body starts to tingle. She can feel the pressure inside her brain. His face looks double to her.

"I love you, I love you," she speaks. Her bottom lip quivers as her body and breasts jerk up and down.

Ray is feeling himself, so he unmercifully pumps faster and harder, giving her his all. His ass pumps up and down as he takes her tongue in his mouth. He allows his dick to run up on her swollen clit.

She utters and moans his name. "*Yes, baby, yes.* Ray, *fuck me fuck me* baby!"

Ray licks her tears with every thrust thereafter. He lifts up, placing his two hands around her neck, cutting off the wind that fills her lungs. Cum rushes from her body. He fucks and fucks, pushing harder, faster like lightning striking over and over. His juices squirt vulgarly through her body. She feels his worth, but he continues to fuck her stroke after stroke, just when she thought he was done.

"Awww! Shit!" he yells as he deposits what feels like a ton of nut inside of her nest egg. Ray slows down, then he lays on top of her, giving her all his weight. He holds on to her as if it's the last time he will see her again.

After about a minute, he kisses her on her soft cheek and rolls over. He lifts his head and looks between her legs. *Just what I thought.* He sees red blood between her legs that covered his white sheets.

"You ok?" He's in a panic. His eyes dart from left to right.

"Yeah. I'm fine. The blood is mine. Ray, I was a virgin."

"A virgin?!"

"Yeah. When you break a virgin in, that's what happens the first time?"

Ray lays back down, relieved he didn't hurt the love of his life. His chest swells up because he's the first man she's ever been with. He looks at the ceiling as he lays beside her, taking hold of her hand.

"Angie. Thanks. From now on, you gon' be my only girl, and that you can count on. And if you want to stop working, you can. I will take care of you no matter what. Just don't ever lie to me or fuck around on me. You gon' be my main boo for life and that you can take to the bank."

How he gon' take care of me? This house was a gift, he says, and he's driving a hooptie, she thinks to herself.

"I love you too," she whispers, curling under him as they fall asleep.

CHAPTER 18

The next morning, Ray and Angie picked up where they left off last night. They make love all morning. Ray is *pussy-matized* and she is *dick-matized*. Ray's so intoxicated that he forgot about him and Poogie's morning meeting. When they're done with their love-making session, they take showers and start all over again. He is on cloud nine. His heart is so into her that he can't see the stars or the moon. All he knows is the sun is shining and he is on top of the world.

Ray's had a lot of women, but never one that sucks such good dick and has such a bomb ass pussy. He's never fucked a virgin. Now he knows why she sucks so many lollipops. The whole time they've been together, he has never fucked Angie. She has only sucked his dick, allowed him to play with her clit, and eat her out. Ray was starting to think that she was one of them holy-rollie chicks.

Ray and Angie dried off and dressed.

"When we gon' get some more rain? The grass is turning brown," she comments, looking out of his large window in the bedroom.

"I know, right," he responds, picking up his cell that reads 12 missed calls. He listens to his messages.

"Where you at, G? It's 12 noon. You was supposed to hit a nigga up at 11, out," Poogie states.

"Fuck, I forgot!" He didn't bother to listen to his other 11 messages. He called his boy right away.

"Hello?" Poogie answers.

"G, damn my bad. Can we meet now?"

"Where you been?"

"I got caught up. My bad, G."

"Meet me at Maxwell's restaurant in about two hours," Poogie orders.

"I'm there. Give me about two and a half or so."

"Later," Poogie says and they end their call.

"Angie, I got some shit to handle this morning. I'ma drop you off. I'ma meet you later tonight."

"Ok, but I can stay here if you want me to."

"Nah, I'll take you home. Won't be goin' through my shit," he jokes.

"Let's go then," she says, feeling some type of way 'cause it seems to her that Ray don't want her in his house alone, as if he's hiding something.

***

Three hours pass. Ray walks in Maxwell's. He locates Poogie.

"What up dough?" They touch fists as Ray takes a seat.

"Dat nigga Shorty Duce hip me to some real shit yesterday."

"Word?"

"Word. He sayin' the streets talkin'."

"About?" Ray petitions.

"About that shit that went down in the trap. They sayin' the five-O got a witness. Some cat named Booman."

"Who dat?"

"Don't know, but Shorty Duce gon' find out."

"Shorty Duce knows?"

"Naw, we was choppin' it up and he just spit that shit my way. So I asked if he know the cat. He was like nah, but his man know'em and the cat been running his chops sayin' he saw two guys coming out that joint gettin' in a blue car and the car didn't move for a minute until the place went up in flames."

"He's accurate as a mufucka. Shit!" Ray lets out, taking a sip of water. "You know what we gotta do?"

"I'm two steps ahead, my nigga," Poogie says.

"Why didn't you tell me dis shit last night?" Ray questions.

"Because last night was yo night, and me and Kim fucked until the fuckin' sun came up."

"G, you wild. You betta be careful fuckin' wit another man's treasure. That's the shit that get most nigga's hairline fractures."

"G, I'on think they seeing eye-to-eye no more." Poogie is being naive.

"She says."

"You know some'em I'on know?" Poogie questions.

"Naw. I pay that business no mind. I still say she's trouble."

"You know what they say though, birds of a feather."

"Naw, G. Angie is nothing like her."

"You say."

"G, I'm out. I picked that package up and made that deposit yesterday." Ray changes the subject.

"How much?" Poogie goes along with it.

"500 Large."

"Ray, we on top of the world, ain't we?"

"And you know dis, but remember: no madder how much money we got or get, the number one rule is to keep humble and stay low."

"Be safe, playa," Poogie says.

"The same to you. You not coming?"

"Nah, I'ma stay. I've been scoping out showdy over there." He circles his eyes and they land towards the bar. "She's looking thick as a snicka." He laughs.

"Boy, you sick," Ray returns, giving his man dap, then exits.

On his way back across town, all he could think about is Angie and how she saved herself for the one true man in her life. He tries to wrap his mind around her falling for him when—to her—he's nobody. An average-ass nigga.

He pulls up to an Audi dealership and hollas at his man Tra, who's the finance manager.

"Hey, G. What brings you through? You tired of driving that old Honda?"

"I'll never get rid of old Bessie. She's been faithful as hell and it's hard to find a faithful bitch." They laugh.

"True dat, man. So what brings you through? You wanna buy a nigga like me some lunch?"

"Nah, man. You not my type. Between my ears and yours, I wanna get that Audi Q7 for this friend of mines."

"*Whew*, you playin' big," Tra teases.

"How much we talkin' fa that bitch?"

"For you, fifty. She's a high class hoe."

"There you go wit that sales talk. You DC niggas, I swear," Ray shoots.

"You know I gotta make a livin' somehow," Tra playfully says, thinking Ray is just window shopping.

Ray leans into Tra's ear. "How about forty cash?"

"You hit the lotto?" Tra is being funny, not knowing Ray is loaded.

"You a real funny dude, but on the real, what up?"

"We can do that." Tra's eyes light up. "Sold. I'ma send my peeps over. Her name is Missy. She gon' cash dat deal."

"Tra, not a word. If I hear anything on them streets, I know my secret wasn't safe." Ray looks at him with a raised eyebrow.

"We good. No worries here. And do come back."

"Fa' sho," Ray adds, taking his cell out his pocket to call Missy (aka Carman).

CHAPTER 19

"Hey, bro, sorry for your loss. Lil man was a good fella for real. If there's anything else I can do for you, just holla," Ray tells Big C as they stand in front of Little Yanks coffin.

"You've done enough. Just the fact that you picked up the tab was like the world to me and my fam," Big C utters.

"That's nutten, man. Anything we can do, just ask," Ray tells him, showing his family some love.

"Yeah man, if it's anything we can do just ask," Poo interjects.

"I didn't know y'all hanging like that." Big C is puzzled.

Ray turns to face Poogie. "Who, Poo? He my main man. You know we go back a long way. My brother used ta hang tight wit'em back in the street times, feel that?"

"I know, we all did back then … we all did, then somehow your brother got popped, then niggas started changing. Look, Ray man, thanks again for coming. I'm gon' holla at the rest of the guests. Ray, thanks again. I'm forever in your doubt."

"Neva that. This one is on the house," Ray tells him.

Big C leans and gives him a hug, whispering in his ear, "Watch who you break bread wit." Then they separate. "Later," Big C says, looking Poogie up and down. Then he walks away.

"What was all dat about?" Ray asks Poogie.

Poogie waves his hand in the air. "Nutten man, that nigga still trippin' about his sister."

But Ray doesn't dismiss it. He puts it to the back of his head for now.

Poogie and Big C's little sister used to date in high school. They were in love—well, she was in love with him. She got pregnant and told Poogie. He asked her, "Who's the father?" She said, "You are," and he said, "I can't be, and if I am you better get rid of it 'cause I ain't got time fo' no little ass brats running around me." This broke her heart because she dreamed of having a life with him. Her family moved her to Washington, DC. She went to college, had the baby, in which he found out about later. But he does not send her one red cent. Big C does. He hates him for that, not to mention the other things, but he minds his business when it comes to his little sister. It's her life, she told him. And he keeps that in mind.

Big C also thinks Poogie snitched their crew out, and that is why Ray's big brother is in prison to this day. Big C just doesn't trust Poogie at all.

CHAPTER 20

It's six in the evening. The sky is dark from the black rain clouds that hover over the sun. The warm breeze is blowing as big raindrops pour from the sky. Lighting flashes as waves of thunder roar.

"Damn, of all days, why did it have to rain today?" Ray asks as he parks his rental on Geist, located on the North side of Indiana. He watches for his prey.

"Bingo." It's seven thirty and his target is on the move. Ray's patience pays off.

Ray starts his car up and turns the corner. He rolls his window down. "Hey G."

His prey walks over to Greet him, not knowing this would be the last day of his life.

Bloc! Bloc!

Ray immediately put two in his chest. His prey drops to the wet ground. Ray jumps out the car. *Bloc, bloc, bloc!*

Three more to the head and two in his stomach.

Ray bends over to see if the man is still breathing. He hears or sees no movement. Ray kisses the man on his check. "This is business. Sorry but I gotta eat." One more kiss on the other side of his check, then Ray hops back in the car and pulls off. When he gets close to the 'hood, he calls Poogie and tells him to meet him at the trap house.

Poogie hears stress in Ray's voice. "We good?" he asks.

"Damn good," Ray tells him and ends the call.

CHAPTER 21

"Good morning and welcome to the Tom Joiner Morning Show. We have Sable with us this morning. She's taking fifteen callers. So if you want to know what's going to happen in your future, then give us a call right now."

Shorty Duce laughs and says, "Now that Sable, she be on point with her stuff. But I'll neva call her. I'on be wantin' to know what gon' happen to my ass. She might tell me some shit like my dick gon' fall off."

"Man, you crazy as hell," Poogie tells him, sitting behind his steering wheel making a right onto Chester Blvd. "Ok, you know the deal. I'ma go around back and you ring the front door bell. When he comes out, make small talk and I'll take it from there."

"Bet dat."

They park two blocks away from the house that they're going to visit this morning. Shorty Duce rings the bell when he thinks Poogie has made it to the back of the house. A man opens the door. "What's up, man? How you know where I live?"

"G, I didn't. I thought this was my boy Chris's house. He gave me this address. Well at least I thought he did."

"What address did he give you? 'Cause ain't nobody named Chris on this block," he tells Shorty Duce.

"You sho? He just moved—"

Pop! Pop! Pop!

The man's wind pipe is cut off from the smoke that fills his lungs. Poogie broke three bullets off in the back of his neck.

"Damn, Joe, you wasn't playin' was you?" Shorty asks, getting his nerves back in tack. Don't get it wrong, Shorty is used to gun smoke, but he just wasn't expected it.

They pull the body back in the house. "Look in the master bedroom closet," Poogie directs. "Why he put his money in here? That's the first place people gon' look, dumb ass," Poogie lets out.

"You think dis here is the end of the rainbow?" Shorty asks Poogie, who is still searching. When he sits up, he sees Shorty holding a bag full of money.

"That'll do, let's go."

They go to the front door, making sure it's locked, but little do they know, someone else is in the house. She saw their faces, and knows their voices.

CHAPTER 22

Ray and Angie are driving down the parkway headed to the mall.

"Ray, can I tell you something from the heart."

Ray gives her a glance. "What up?"

"I love you so much. I mean you have really changed my—"

Bang. Ray's car is hit from behind. *Bang!* Hander this time.

"What he fuck?!" Ray whimpers.

"What's going on? Ray, pull over pull over!" Angie order in a voice of panic.

Bang! Bang! The car behind him rams into his car again. This time Angie's legs start to shake. Ray puts the pedal to the metal.

"Angie, call Poo!" Ray shouts as he races down the freeway. "Call poo now!" he shouts again.

But she's in twilight zone.

"Angie! Angie!" Ray calls out again and again.

He crashes into a car in passing. Then his right tire hits the side of the road. He's moving fast as the car behind him gains on him. His back tire comes off.

He looks over at Angie who is in shock.

Then he turns into a Mall parking lot where lots of people are walking. He pulls into a parking space but the car behind him is still giving chase. They pull behind him, Ray grabs his Desert Eagle from under his seat and quickly jumps out the car, hits the ground and rolls.

Bloc, Bloc, Bloc! is all Angie is hearing. Then she feels a jerk on her arm. She knows she's being thrown into another car. She feels the car moving. She's crying and shaking.

Moments later she feels herself being lifted out the car and taken into a house. She's lowered on a sofa.

"Angie, Angie, can you hear me?" she faintly hears. Her body starts to shake and shake more.

"I can't believe this shit," Ray says out loud to himself. He puts in a call to Poo.

"Hello?" Poo answers.

"Poo man, I need you. I need you to meet me at Dijon's Spaghetti House."

"What?"

"Man, just meet me," he tells Poogie.

"Ok, but you sound flexed, you a'ight?" Poogie asks.

"Nah, I'll tell you then. Meet me in about 2 hours."

"I'm there," Poogie shouts back.

Then Ray puts in a call to Carman.

"Carman look, meet me at that Spanish joint, Fredonia Foods Mart?

"What time?" she says with no questions asked.

"At 5pm."

"And you know I'll be there. I hear it in your voice something's wrong so I'll see you then, I guess," she tells him.

"SHIT!" he lets out when he turns seeing Angie in a trance.

"What happened?" she mumbles softly,

"We got in a car accident," he tells her.

"No, somebody ... somebody was chasing us. Who, what?" she asks as she starts to come to.

"Look bae, I gotta go take care of something real quick. You stay here. You're safe."

"Where are we?"

"We at one of my other houses that no one knows about. This man that was parked beside us brought us home. Some cats got shot up in the parking lot. Bae, I had to do what I had to do." He looks her in her eyes and says, "So you stay here. No one will come here. I gotta go and see what that shit was all about."

"Ray, please watch out and be safe. And thanks for saving my life. I love you so much."

"I hear dat but Bae I gotta go."

"Ok, I'll stay put."

Ray walks to his garage, gets in one of his cars, presses the button for the garage door to open then races off.

CHAPTER 23

"Man, do you know who them niggas could've been? I mean I ain't neva seen them. What side of the street they playing on?" Ray is asking Poo, who seems to be clueless.

"Nah man, I can't call it. I mean, do you know what they look like at all? The plates to their car and shit?" Poo is asking Ray, who is sitting behind the steering wheel of his car.

"Nope. All I know is they was tryna run a nigga down," Ray lies to his boy, not trusting anyone at this point in the game. He's remembering what Big C said at the funeral in his ear.

"G, that was deep. Do you think Angie know who they was?" Poo is still curious.

"Naw, G, she was too shacked up to see anything. I just told her it was a police chase. She was out of it. She's so green that bitch don't know shit."

Poo looks at Ray curiously.

Ray looks at him. "What's wrong wit' you?"

"You called the love of yo life a bitch. I mean that's funny now so what's up wit dat shit? I guess the perfect lady done pissed you off. I guess birds of a feather do run together, some shit like that, huh?" Poo throws in his face.

"G, my life was on the line. I asked her to call you but she was so shocked. I need a down bitch, one that knows the game, one that has my back when shit gets fucked up. Right now my life is out of order. Somebody is gunning for me and I'on know who the hell it is. I really need to make some real sense of all this. This shit right here just got real," Ray spits.

Poogie is looking out the window. "I hear you loud and clear," he says with thoughts of his own.

CHAPTER 24

3 Days After The Shootout

Ray pulls up to his driveway in Oak Brook. He notices an unfamiliar car parked in front of his house. He gets out his car with precaution. The door opens to the Porsche Boxster.

"Hey you," Angie greets with a smile, closing the door of her new Porsche.

Ray is taken back. "Whose whip you flossing?" he asks her.

"Mines ... you like?"

"I love you doing it big fa' sho."

"It ain't like that. I wish. The company bought it for me because I was the top salesperson two years in a row. You wanna go for a spin?"

"Yeah, but not the spin you talkin' 'bout," he tells her, pulling her into his arms.

"You so nasty."

"Born that way." He gets jazzy.

They head in the house. She cooks them something to eat then she smashes him off with some good, good. As they lay in the bed, Ray notices blood on his sheets again.

"You still bleedin?"

She looks between her legs. "I guess it's 'gon take a while to get used to that monster size dick you got," she jokes.

"Y'all women go through it. I'm just glad God made me a man."

"I'm glad too, 'cause if you was a girl, I would be gay," she teases.

"I know that's right," he lets out. "Bae, I gotta go meet Bruce today."

"Bruce? I thought he was out of town for a week."

Ray looks over at her with his lips turned up. "How would you know dat?"

"Oh, um, I overheard Kim sayin' it."

"How would she know?" he quizzes.

"Your guess is as good as mines. Now enough wit' the questions. Let mommy take care of daddy." She takes him in her mouth and it's on from there.

CHAPTER 25

Four Months Later

Ray drives to the Bank of Trust. He can't help but think about Angie, the love of his life. He bought her an Audi Q7. He wasn't going to give it to her after she showed up at his house four months ago with a new sports car, but he thought, *What the hell. She'll either drive it or let it sit.* When he gave it to her, she was so happy she acted as if it was her first car. She drives it to his house every time she comes over. She is so appreciative and he loves her for that.

He retrieves his cell and enters her number before entering the bank, but it goes straight to voicemail.

"Hey, it's yo boy," Ray says. "When you get this, holla back. We need to talk." After leaving her that message, he cuts his phone off, turns his engine off, gets out and walks into the bank. He steps to the help desk.

"Hey, I'm here to see Mr. Black."

"Is he expecting you today, or is there something I can help you with?" the lady behind the desk asks.

As fine as you are, hell, it's a lot you can help me with, he thinks.

"No, I really need to see him."

"Ok, I'll check to see if he will see you today. What's your name?" She picks up her phone. When she is done, she looks up at Ray, who is patiently waiting in front of her.

"Sir, if you will have a seat in the lobby, he will be with you momentarily."

"Thanks." As he walks away, she looks him over. *That muthafucka looks like Morris Chestnut. He is fine as shit!*

He takes a seat in the lobby and reads magazines to pass time.

One hour later ...

"Hi, son. What can I do for you today?" Mr. Black walks up to Ray and asks.

Ray stands and shakes Mr. Black's hand.

"Sir, I would like to do business with you. Since Youngbleed was gunned down, may he rest in peace, I ain't got no connect, you feel me? He told me you was his man, no disrespect. This a little before he got knocked. He said he was gon' introduce us because he was thinking about bowing to the game since his boy got smoked one month before him. Sir, I have nowhere to turn and my product is getting low," Ray covers his mouth, whispering so no one could read his lips.

Mr. Black scans Ray's face. "Come with me, son."

Ray obeys, following Mr. Black to a side room. They enter and Mr. Black closes the oversized door behind them.

"Look, nigga. Don't you ever come in my establishment lyin' to me. Neva! I know all about you. Bleed told me you was buyin' from him. If that nigga was tryna get ghost, he would have told me." Mr. Black pulls his heat from his suit jacket and steps back, pointing it in Ray's direction.

Ray stays calm, cool, and collected. He takes his stand, tilts his hat to the side with his toothpick hanging out of his mouth.

"G, dis shit is real. Now if you wanna turn shit up, we can do dat. Fear don't know my bloodline. I didn't come in here to bring the heat. I come to you as a businessman. A street nigga, the only way I know how. Now we can take these streets over or can die tryin'. 'Cause one things fo' sho', I'ma try 'cause it's the only life I know," Ray tells him.

Mr. Black lowers his hammer. "You can never be too careful. I'm sorry, son. So what you talking?"

"A hunnid."

"A hundred bricks?"

"You got it," Ray tells him.

Mr. Black pulls out a pen and a sticky note. He jots down the pickup and the drop offs with the times and hands it to Ray.

"Come here and deposit the money in this name and pick up the product at this address. It will be in the blue mailbox on the corner. Make sure you go and get it at this time because this is the only window of time them pigs giving me."

Ray reads the sticky note. "12 midnight, every Tuesday, Erica Flood, and 12G's a brick. Got that," Ray says, handing the sticky note back to Mr. Black.

"I like your style, son."

Ray says nothing else. He got what he came for. He nods and makes and about face and heads out the door from which he entered, leading him outside into the pouring rain.

CHAPTER 26

"Carman, where you get this car from?" Kim asks her.

"My boo."

"Damn, you flossing these days. New clothes, jewels, now a big body BMW, drop top. Where they do that at?" Kim's puzzled.

"Well, I got a new boo and he's taking care of a fat bitch. You jelly?"

"Neva. And what's this new boo name? Maybe I know him. And if I don't, he got any friends or brothers?"

"You'on know'em. And I told myself I wasn't gon let nobody in our business. He is all mines and that's gon' be that. 'Cause I see how you be eyeing Ray and you know he fuckin' wit' yo girl Angie," Carman tells her.

"Whateva. Whoeva he is probably using yo fat ass anyway. You probably running dope fo' his ass and this yo pay."

"You just lemon lime 'cause I'm gettin' it and you not." Carman turns her nose up at her, rubbing on her thickness. "Well I gotta go, ain't got time for small talk. A bitch is moving."

"Movin'? Where you movin'?" Kim asks.

"He bought a bitch a condo in Indi."

"How I'ma see you from now on? I know you gon' give me the address," Kim says.

"Hell no! You will never know where I lay my head, bitch. Yo ass is scandalous," Carman tells her, walking into their apartment building to wait for the moving company.

"That bitch, she lyin'. Don't nobody want her 300-pound ass. Who would stick they dick in that?" Kim asks herself as she sits on her porch drinking her yoo-hoo.

CHAPTER 27

Four Days Earlier

Bruce is in Indi, chopping it up with his new boy Zack Randolph, who plays for Memphis. They are hanging out on 40th street.

"I got five on it, bro," Zack spits, bending over holding two dice in his hand.

"Put it where yo mouth is, nigga," one of the men snap, standing around in the craps circle.

"You ain't said shit, G," Bruce chimes in, throwing 5 G's in the middle of the circle on the floor.

Two hours pass and Zack and Bruce are making a killing. They gather their winnings so they can bounce.

"So that's how y'all gon do? Y'all ain't gon' let niggas get back?" Johnny boy lets out.

"Bro, y'all ain't shit," one of the losers add.

"Call us what you want but you won't call us broke," Zack states with a chuckle.

J.J. Jackson

Bruce and Zack walk out the hall with their ladies.

Bruce never notices Mac-Ten standing on the side. Mac-Ten places a call to his boy Ray, but he gets his voice-mail on the first ring. He makes a mental note to call him later to tell him what he just saw with his own eyes.

CHAPTER 28

It's April and the sun is blazing at an abnormal 99 degrees. Ray is pulling into his driveway of his house in Oak Brook where Angie awaits him. He gets out his car and she does the same. They greet one another with a kiss.

"Angie, we need to talk," he tells her.

"Ok, babe, shoot."

"Let's go in the house first." They walk in the house and get settled. When they sit down to watch TV, he starts talking.

"Bae, we been seeing each other for a while. I love you and I feel you really love me, right?"

"That's right," she says, feeling a little uneasy as to what he's going to say next.

"It's something you need to know about yo man."

She adjusts her body. "I'm listening."

"Angie, I don't own half of Rogers. I'm a boss nigga." He waits for her reaction.

"Boy you silly. I knew that."

"How you know?" He feels relieved.

"I didn't know you was selling drugs, but I knew you wasn't half owner of Rogers. Hell, old man Rogers live in an oak house but this is a mansion. I know ain't nobody just up and give you this shit, but it was yo lie and I was gon' let you have it. A bitch is green, but I'm not that fuckin' green."

He gazes in her eyes. "So you down wit' it?"

"Yeah, what you do is what you do. I love you for you, not what you can do for me."

He moves her legs off him, lifts up, bends on one knee in front of her, pulls a small black box out his pocket and opens it.

"Oh hell ... what you gon' ask ...? God no!" She starts crying.

"Angie Green, will you do me the honor of becoming Angie Poole?"

"Hell yeah! Yes, yes!" She jumps up and hugs him around his neck. He kisses her and takes her by her hand.

"C'mere."

She follows him to the garage door. He unlocks it with a key. When he opens the door, her mouth drops open.

"Oh shit! Oh my God. Look at all these cars." She walks in and passes car after car.

Porsche 911, custom made Benz, Range Rover, Lincoln, Cadillac Escalade truck and sports car, convertible Corvette, 1967 Stingray coupe and his baby the Italia Ferrari 458.

"Ray, yo ass is the muthafuckin' boss of bosses. When do yo drive all these?"

"Oh, best believe they get they work in," he tells her, smiling.

"Kim said she thought y'all niggas was on the low, but bae said Shorty Duce never said anything like that to her when they pillow talk."

"Babe, we gotta keep dis here between your eyes, ears, and mines. It's gon' be lots of shit you may see or hear but you gotta say nothing to no one and the number one rule is: if the pigs come, you don't know shit. Neva show fear to them or no one. That is the life of a gangster's wife," he explains.

"I know, I know."

"No, don't know. *Learn and listen.* I got a 100K lawyer, that's what I pay him for, his mouthpiece, not yours, not mines, his. So if them pigs come yo way, no matter what they say, how much time they say you can get or what they gon' do to me or your fam. Know we covered and keep your mouth shut. No words. Let them do the talking and when they done playin' good cop, bad cop, you look up at 'em and say you want to talk to your lawyer. Now, is this the life you willing to lay down fa?" he asks her with a serious face.

She hesitates for a second. "Yes, I'm willing to lay down my life for you, the one and only man I have ever loved."

She starts taking off her clothes piece by piece. Then she takes her pointer finger and motions him to come to her.

"Come get your pussy 'cause we hungry," she tells him, pointing to her kitty kat.

A grin crosses his face as he walks over to her. He's more than happy to feed her and her kitty.

CHAPTER 29

Angie and Ray are at Earl Banisters shop on Eutaw Street in Baltimore, Maryland. Angie insisted on Earl making the clothes for their wedding. Ray didn't want to put up a fight, so he booked a private jet to Maryland.

She is being fitted for her wedding dress in one room and he is being fitted for his tux in another. He is a little frazzled because he's in unknown territory without his bagger, so he wants this over so he can get back to Chicago. When they are done, they all sit in the room making small talk and listening to Angie go on and on about her plans for the wedding.

Buzz, Buzz! is the sound of Ray's cell.

"Give me a sec." He walks to another room to talk.

"Hey G, what up dough?" he answers, knowing who it is.

"I can't call it. Shit, Kim is in the ATL at her mom's so a nigga solo. But I got good news."

"Spit."

"Shorty Duce took care of that package in Indi for us," Poogie tells him.

"Shorty Duce?! Shorty Duce?! I thought we wasn't using him for shit. I'm baffled," Ray tells his boy.

"We not. I just told him to do me a favor and he was happy to prove his loyalty."

"You suppose to take care of it. Not him. If that nigga gets caught up, what we gon' do? 'Cause you know he gon' talk. Don't you?"

"Chill, Joe, he ain't gon' do shit. That nigga got too much respect to do that shit to me."

"G, it ain't all about you. We one, and that nigga gon' snitch sho as his name is Rick Smith, Jr. That nigga told on me in school after I beat the brakes off his ass, so I know if them letter boys get at his punk ass, we goin' down—and that shit there is *real*."

"So what you want me ta do? Bottom his ass?" Poogie asks.

"Whateva it takes. They make caskets for friends too," Ray bucks.

Poogie raises up out his chair. "Look, G. That's my boy, ain't nobody gon' touch that dude. He did me a favor so I'm asking you as a man, a partna, to give that nigga a pass."

"What happened to no eyes left open, huh?" Ray is heated.

Poogie chokes up 'cause that was his rule, not Ray's. "I hear you but let's think clear here. This is some'em I ordered. We in this shit together, so if one goes, we all go. And I ain't tryna go. I put my life on that shit there. I do," Poogie pleads his case for his man.

"I remember you puttin' yo life on them niggas in Gangstaville. You do remember that?" Ray reminds him.

Poogie is scared for his boy's life. He knows all too well how Ray gets down and he feels like he put him in this position to choose to let Shorty Duce live or die.

"A'ight man, do what yo gotta do but know it's your move and my hands are clean of any bloodshed," Poogie says.

Ray becomes silent, not believing his right hand is not backing him on this one. "I'll let him live for now," he says finally.

"Ok G, thanks." Poogie is relieved and grateful at the same time. Ray just don't know the load he just took off Poogie's shoulders.

"Don't thank me just yet. I just hope yo ass right. I gotta get back to this wedding planning shit. I'll holla when I touch down," Ray says and ends the call with a bad feeling in his gut.

That shit was close, Poogie says to his self.

Ray walks back in the room where Angie and the others are sitting talking. She looks over at her boo.

"Is all well in the neighborhood?" she asked

"I'm good. Who was you on the phone wit?" he asks her.

How the fuck he know I was on the phone? she thinks. *This nigga got eyes in the back of his head.*

"Kim called. She just wanted to know when I was coming back. I told her tomorrow."

"Oh, where she at?" he quizzes.

"You know her ass is in the 'hood sittin' on the porch."

Now why did she lie, 'cause Poogie just told me she was in Atlanta at her moms and shit?

He musters a response. "I know that's right."

"Ray, babe, when we get back I've gotta go to my mother's for about two or three days. But I'll be back."

"Oh, you want me to go wit' you?"

"Nah, I'm a big girl. I can make this trip to Indi by myself."

"If you say so."

Ray doesn't want to question her. He just makes a mental note of her lie and brushes it off until later. His mind is too far gone and he wants to get back to Chi-Town like yesterday.

CHAPTER 30

Ray and Angie are riding home from the airport and his gray cell rings. He takes a look at the number. *Who dis?* The number doesn't serve his dome, but it's his private line so he answers.

"Holla at yo boy," he greets.

"Yooo ... son, where you been?" Mac-Ten asks.

"Around, what up witcha?" Ray returns.

"Can you talk?"

"You got it."

"Son, it's like this. I've been tryna catch up with you for a minute. I holla'd at yo man Poo, but I guess he forgot to tell you ta hit me up."

"He musta, but you got me, now spit," Ray commands.

"Yo son, it's like dis. I was on 40th in Indi at the crap spot, kickin' it wit my man Gusman, right. So it was these two cats in the joint winning loot like it wasn't shit, so I takes notice. Low and behold it was your boy Bruce."

"What?! What dat G doin' in Indi?"

"My exact words. He was hangin' wit that cat that plays for Memphis. Zack Randolph."

"I'm with you, keep going," Ray tells him, wanting this nigga to get to the point.

"Well, when they left they took two broads wit' em and you will neva guess who was tonguing him down."

"Nah, enlighten me."

"Sorry to lay this shit on you but it was yo bitch Angie."

Ray's heart starts to pound against his chest. His head is spinning. He feels like he's losing his breath. But he remains cool.

"You sure, G?"

"On er' thing I love. Son, I had ta tell you. I couldn't see you go out like dat. Son, I've been in yo same shoes. These bitches ain't loyal," Mac-Ten claims.

"You know if this shit don't pan out, I'm gunnin' fo' you. And if it does, thanks G for savin' my life. I owe you one."

"Oh, it will and you welcome."

Ray ends that call and dials another. Angie sits on the passengers seat wondering what he was talking about on the phone.

"Hello?" the person answers.

"Hey man, dis me Ray."

"Hello, Ray. What can I do for you?" Private Investigator Williams asks.

"Can you meet me at about seven tonight at yo office?"

"I sure can," he answers, all chipper.

"A'ight, see you then."

"Okay."

Ray hangs up the phone.

"Is everything okay?" Angie asks. "You look kinda flustered?"

"Oh yeah, babe. Just fine, little some'em I need to take care of. Nutten yo man can't handle. He flashes her a fake smile, then glues his eyeballs back on the road the whole way home. She feels the tension but she decides not to push it.

CHAPTER 31

2 Weeks Pass

Shorty Duce is driving down highway 90. He hears sirens behind him. Looking in his rearview mirror, he pulls over to the shoulder hoping the police car will pass him by, but lady luck isn't with him this day.

"Shit! What this pig want?" he whispers, getting his credentials ready.

After about what seems like forever, the hog steps his fat, short ass out of his car. He walks up behind Shorty's driver side door and leans over.

"License, insurance, registration, sir."

Shorty has it all handy. He hands the officer the information that he requests. "What you stop me for, sir?"

"You have a broken tail light."

"Really? I didn't know."

"Well now you do." The short fucka gets smarts. "Sit tight," he adds as he walks back to his squad car. When he comes back: "Sir, can you step out of the car please?"

"Why?"

"Because I say so."

"Yoo, this some bullshit!" Shorty says as he steps out his car. When he's completely out of the car, he sees two more squad cars pull up.

"What I do?" he asks the man as he turns him around, slamming him against the car to handcuff him and body search his ass.

"Nothing today, my man. It's what you didn't do. You have an outstanding warrant for child support."

"What? I paid it." Shorty directs his attention to the black officer that just walked up.

"Tell it to the judge," the black officer says.

"Sell out!" Shorty blurts out. "What about my ride?"

"We'll have it towed," the fat white officer tells him.

"Towed?! Towed?! This a Lotus. You can't just tow a fuckin' Lotus!" Shorty shouts.

"Well, we can have Mr. Sellout over here drive it to the station if you'd like, but either way, it's going to the station. Or it can sit here as far as I'm concerned," the white officer shoots.

"You hatin' bitch ass cracka!"

"Whateva, but I'm not the cracka that forgot to pay his child support, am I?"

"And don't drop the fuckin' soap," the black officer chimes in.

A female officer does an illegal search of his vehicle while Shorty sits in the squad car.

"Bingo! We got a gun," she says out loud, and it's loaded. "Bingo, we got four nice sized bricks and it looks like coke to me. What you think, Jones?" she asks the other officer who is standing by the car, writing something down. He looks at Shorty and shakes his head and smiles. The black officer gets the test kit out and tests the brick to see what it is.

"It's coke, alright. Pure coke."

"Well, my friend. It looks like we gotcha. Watch your head," he tells him as he closes the door to the squad car.

Shorty is vexed. *How the fuck did they find the damn secret compartment? Fuck! Somebody set my ass up. Who knew about the damn compartment?*

The lady officer sticks her head through the squad car window.

"Next time you get a hiding spot built in your car, hire my man. Your black button sticks out like a sore thumb. My man would have hooked you the fuck up," she tells him, laughing.

CHAPTER 32

When they pull up to the station, Shorty Duce demands his one, free unrecorded phone call.

"When they're done processing you, they'll let you make a call," the transporting officer tells him.

They process him in and let him make his one call. He dials his one and only boo.

"Bey, look, five-O got my ass."

"What?! Why? When?" She is full of questions.

"Look, I'll tell you later. But for now I need you to find a good lawyer and a good bail bondsman."

"Ok, boo, I'ma call one now and I'll be right there. Where is the money for bond and how much is it?"

"It's in the oven under the burner, wrapped in aluminum foil, but they haven't set a bond yet."

"In the oven?! Boy, you crazy? Suppose I decided to cook or some'em?"

"Girl, you can't cook rice."

They laugh.

"Whateva, call me when they set the bond."

"That's my girl," he says, then he hangs up.

The officer puts him in a holding cell. Lucky for Shorty, this is a slow night; it's only two others in the cramped cold cell.

***

"Mr. Watts, you're free to go," the officer says, opening the holding cell that's located a few cells down from Shorty's cell.

Big C walks out and becomes a free man for tonight. When he gets to his car, he calls Ray right away.

"Wussup, C?" Ray answers.

"You, man. Get dis shit, I just got outta the joint. They got me on some DUI bullshit right, but my chick bailed me out. Hear dis though, that nigga Shorty Duce in dat joint as we speak."

"I'm listening," Ray says.

"G, they got his ass on three kilos and a lock and loaded. I heard five-O talkin' 'bout that shit when they was gettin' my release papers ready."

Ray is vexed. *I told Poogie this shit would happen.*

"Did he see you?"

"Naw, I was in another holding cell, but get dis, they talkin' the big boys. They say they was puttin' in a call to them Fed crack asses. Watch yo back, 'cause I know that's your man's boy and all ... but dat nigga 'bout to turn hot. I could feel that shit in my bones when I passed his cell. That nigga was scared as shit," Big C informs.

"Good looking, G."

"It's whateva man, you was there fa my moms and shit, and man, you paid fo' my little brother's funeral. I owe you big time."

"Man, that was some short shit. That there is a given," Ray tells him.

"You got dat, G. Hit me if you eva need anything, I mean anything," Big C lets out before ending their call.

Ray is so pissed he doesn't know what to do. As he thinks of his next move, his phone vibrates again.

"What is it now?" he says out loud to himself as he looks at the caller ID. "Dis me," he greets.

"Hey, I got what you asked for. How far away are you?"

"About 25 minutes out."

"Ok, I'll be here in my office unless you wanna wait until tomorrow?"

"Nah, I'll be there, hold tight," Ray tells him.

Ray ends the call with the P.I. and makes a U-turn, hoping Mac-Ten was wrong.

Fifteen minutes later he's pulling up in the P.I.'s lot. He parks his truck in the back, gets out, jogs up the steps then enters the office.

147

"Hey man, got here as soon as I could," Ray tells him a little out of breath.

"Damn my man, you musta been flying. You said 25 minutes out," the P.I. jokes, but Ray isn't in the mood for small talk.

"Some'em like dat. So what you got for a nigga?" Ray gets to the point.

Mr. Williams hands Ray the pictures in a large, white envelope. Ray sifts through them all, getting the same results, picture after picture. His head becomes heavy so he sits while continuing to look, and look, and look at the pictures of his wife-to-be fucking his boy Bruce in the shower, on the floor, in her car. She's even sucking his dick, he's eating her pussy, they're out on the town. Lots of pictures of them at parties, restaurants, even pictures of Bruce's grandmother and her shopping as if it is Bruce she's going to marry.

Ray gazes at the pictures a little while longer, then he looks up at Mr. Williams with puppy eyes.

"Good work." He hands him a fat envelope and slowly walks towards the door to leave.

"Ray, if …"

Ray puts his hand up, cutting Mr. Williams off mid-sentence as he continues to look at the evidence that's before him.

***

Shorty Duce is worried about his charges.

"I can't go back to jail. Hell, I know I can't do prison," he says to himself as he paces his bedroom floor.

"I can rat that nigga Poogie out. I know he doing weight wit' Ray. I hate Ray any way shit. I can tell 'bout Mac-Ten killing that nigga not too long ago for Poogie. Yeah that'a do it!"

He reaches for his cell and the card that lays on his nightstand. He smiles and dials the leading detective on his case.

CHAPTER 33

"Hi, bae," Angie greets her man as she walks in his house.

"Hey you." Ray wraps his arms around her waist as if he knows nothing.

"It smells good in here, what you up to?"

"It's your favorite—scallops, shrimp with some fresh spinach salad on the side, wit' red wine," Ray tells her with a smile whipped on his face.

"Woo! Now that's what a woman needs in her life, a man that can cook. I hit the lotto fa real," she says jokingly.

"I know you did. So how was work, bae?" he asks, breaking their embrace, walking back to the kitchen to prepare their plates.

"It was just that—work. You know, same ole same ole," she tells him while washing her hands then taking a seat at the table.

"Did you make any sales?"

"As a matter of fact, yes. I picked up four new companies."

"That's funny 'cause I went past your office to take you to lunch, the receptionist told me you was on vacation or some shit like dat."

With a turned up face Angie hesitates. She was about to put her glass of wine between her parched lips. She sets the glass back on the table.

"I was on vacation? She's crazy, she musta forgot that I was working out of the downtown office this week."

"You know how that goes. What can you expect from somebody that's making her type of money? You know they make mistakes all the time," he says, putting the plates on the table, taking his seat right beside her. "Ok, bless the table, I'm hungry," he adds.

"You say it, bae," she insists.

They bow their heads, holding hands.

"God, thank you for this food, my life, my family. God, thank you for who you are and most of all thank you for my beautiful wife-to-be and for the little bambino in her oven. Amen."

Angie immediately opens her eyes.

"How did you find out? How you know?"

He turns and faces her. "How wouldn't I know? Angie, this here is my town. Do you know who you fuckin' wit?"

She nods her head like a child that just got caught with her hand in the cookie jar.

"I ... I was gon' to tell you but I wanted the moment to be right," she says as Teena Marie's "Déjà vu" plays softly in the background.

"So when was the right time gonna come? Enlighten me, please. 'Cause a nigga like me puzzled. I mean you 'bout five months, right?"

"Ray, it's been so much going on with the wedding, you leaving two and three days at a time. Your mood swings. I just didn't know how you was going to take it, that's all, nothing else."

"You funny, Angie, real funny. But it's one thing I do know—after we eat, we goin' to the doctor's office. He gon' do a DNA on the baby."

"A what?! On the what?! Boy, you crazy, see that's why I didn't wanna tell yo ass 'cause of shit like this. I'on know why I got caught up wit' yo ass. An old street nigga. My friends told me not to fuck wit' yo good for nothing ass. I should've known betta. What was I thinking?" she yells in his face.

He stops eating, examines her eyes.

"A street nigga, huh? But it was all Fendi when I gave you stacks on stacks er' day or when you went on shopping sprees, or when this street nigga breakin' pipe off in yo ass. Wait a minute, how about when dis street nigga gave you that 12ct ring you showing off to them same bitch ass friends that told you not to fuck wit me, while all along they tryna get in where they fit in. Now should I go on?"

"Ray, I didn't ask for all this! I got my own job! I was takin' care of me before all this! Know that!" she turns up the heat, shouting and points to herself.

"I bet you was," he says calmly, picking up his fork. He starts eating his food. "I know what we ain't gon' do. We ain't gon' sit here and go back and forth. We gon' eat this good ass meal, then we gon' make that appointment 'cause you already know my get down. So you can yell all you want, but at the end of the day you taking that test."

"I'm not taking shit!"

Ray puts his fork down, slides his chair back, gets up, wraps his manly hands around her tiny neck and commences to choke the living shit outta her. She's kicking and gagging, trying to get air to her lungs.

"You gon' do what the fuck I tell yo little ass to do. Now you gon' go wit' me or I'll be giving yo peeps money to pay the undertaker, your choice." He releases the strong grip he has on her neck, then takes a seat to finish his food.

She looks down at the food in front of her, picks her fork up and starts playing in it as she rubs her neck.

I hope he is the father, 'cause me and Rico, my ex, been using condoms. I knew I should've went over his house that day, but I was mad at Ray I wanted to pay him back. Why did I do it? This nigga is crazy. If he finds out Rico and me been fucking around my ass and his is as good as dead, she's thinking as she rolls the fork around in her food.

Ray glances over at her. "It's your favorite, so eat up. We gotta be at the doc's office in one hour, bae," he tells her as if he never choked the shit outta her.

She starts stuffing food down her sore throat. In between eating, she looks over at Ray. "Ray, can I ask you something?"

"Sure, anything," he says, sucking the food out his teeth.

"Why do you want a DNA test? You think I'm cheating?"

"You's a really funny character. You should have been born in Cali somewhere. They could use somebody like you. We got 45 minutes left so you gon' eat or are you done, 'cause I'm done."

She continues to play in her food, trying to buy time. She's also thinking, *How did I allow myself to get involved with a bipolar nigga? Or maybe he's just an outright psycho.*

CHAPTER 34

Two Weeks Out

"Mr. Poole, you told me to call you and only you when the test results came back."

"That I did. So what's the results?" Ray asks.

"Sir, I don't like doing this over the phone, but in this case I am. Sorry to inform you, the test shows that you're not the father of Ms. Green's unborn."

"Thanks, Doc. Did you get the envelope I dropped off last week?"

"Yes, I did. Thanks again, but that was not necessary."

"I just wanted to give you a little something for going the extra mile. You said it would take six weeks, but you said you would rush it and make it two weeks. So I just wanted to show my gratitude," Ray tells him.

"That was nothing, that's my job. We just happen to have a lab next door and I called in a favor."

"Again, thanks and have a good day," Ray tells him, showing no emotions.

"Sir, I'm sorry for the bad news."

"Don't be, it's not your life that's on the line."

The doctor goes mute, as the line turns cold.

"Hello, hello? Are you still there?" the doctor asks. When he gets no reply, he observes the receiver, hunches his shoulders and hangs up.

"That bird ass bitch. And she had the nerve to be with my main man. That nigga was like a brother to me. That hoe ass bitch!" Ray rants and raves, making a U-turn, dialing his man up who answers on the first ring.

"Sup?" Poogie answers while in the middle of playing a game of bones.

"G, I gotta put in some work so I'ma be off line for a few. If you really need me beep."

"Put in work? You need me to ride out witcha?" Poogie's concerned since he doesn't know what's going on.

"Naw, I'm good. Dis here some personal shit. You been past the spots?"

"You know it, and er' thing is copasetic," Poogie assures.

"That's what's up. Shit G, I been wrapped up in my personal shit, that I almost forgot that nigga Shorty. I hear he's out on these streets. How is that possible, given the charges?" Ray probes.

"I was gon' hit yo ears with that. He came over and told me. Bey bailed him out. He was like, at first they wasn't tryna hear no bail shit but she got him a fat ass lawyer and he got the job done. You know how dat shit goes."

"Nah, maybe you can try explaining it to a nigga like myself." Ray's listening.

"That's history, and I guess he's stickin' to that shit. He seemed real about the shit. I believe'em."

My man is blinded by friendship. Number two rule, trust no man, Ray thinks to himself.

"So when is his court date?" Ray asks.

"He ain't say." Poogie rubs his head.

I bet he didn't, Ray is thinking before he speaks his mind. "That shit didn't strike you as odd? Most niggas get popped, they make bail then they call they man's and tell them all about it, especially when the fuckin' judgment day gone be," Ray explains.

"So you'on spit shit about that Booman situation?"

"C'mon G, you gotta wake up earlier than that."

"A'ight, I'ma holla."

"Later." Poogie is feeling uneasy about the situation, but he dismisses it as Ray being Ray.

Ray ends the call with his man, thinking about how he's gon' have to kill his man's boy. But to be sure of his thoughts about all that's going on, he puts in a call to Kim, the 'hood's earpiece. She answers the phone with excitement.

"Hello!"

"Hey Kim, dis here is Ray."

"I know who it is. I'm just surprised to see it's you. What's poppin'?"

"Can you meet me at Harold's Chicken?"

"What time?" she implores.

"In about two hours."

"A'ight, I'll see you there."

"Don't be late, shawdy."

"Oh, I won't be, trust me," she says with seduction in her voice.

***

Two hours pass. Ray walks in the spot scanning the joint for Kim. His eyes zoom in on her. *Look at this bitch all dolled up*, he thinks, chuckling as he makes his way over to her.

"Hey boo."

"Boo? Boo is for niggas that you'on know, or for the ones you love. You know me and I'm not your lover, so it's Ray to you," he dishes out coldly.

"Whateva," she affirms, picking up her glass of water to wash down the embarrassment that's stuck in her throat.

Ray takes a seat, sliding his sunshades from his face. "Kim, I'ma ask you some questions and I betta not hear nutten I ask you on these streets, you heard?"

"Spit, or foreva hold yo tongue."

"It's about Angie."

She looks at him for a minute. "I'm down."

"I knew you would be, that's why I called you. The first time me and ol' girl fucked, she told me she was a virgin."

"A what? That bitch ain't no virgin. All them niggas she's been fuckin' with ... Did your stupid ass look for blood between them thighs? When you break a virgin in, her ass sho nuff bleeds," she explains to him.

"She did that."

Kim busts out laughing.

"What's so damn funny?"

"You, nigga. You grew up in the Wild Hunnids and you don't know that' the oldest trick in the book?"

"Trick? What trick?" He's lost.

"Let me school yo dumb ass. See, that's why y'all good fellas need to stay wit' us 'hood bitches and leave them suburb birds where they stand. At least wit' us you know what we on—them green backs and a good come-up. Any who, let the lesson begin. Mr. Boss Man, it was probably her time of the month. She fucked you on the first day, so a little blood would come down, just enough to hit them sheets. Now let me ask you: When you fucked again, did she bleed?"

"Yeah, I think so. Like the next day."

"Ta-dah! She was on her joint. Most women don't bleed again unless you holding, like yo man Poogie. Are you hung like him?" She is smiling.

"You'll never know, and I don't be looking at my man's shit. Disrespect me again," he threatens her. "So you still fuckin' my mans?" he asks.

"Hell nah, he ain't gon' fuck my money maka up!"

"You's a funny broad." He grins and stands, then takes a sip of water. He pulls off two bands, throws them on the table. "One more thing. Did Bey mention anything about Shorty Duce getting popped?"

"Yeah, she said she had to go bail his ass out. She said the streets gon' be on lock real soon though."

He looks down at the two bands he threw on the table, digs in his pocket and adds another one. "That should take care of the bill and yo silence."

"It sho will, thanks," she tells him, rolling her eyes, snatching the money up.

Ray just shakes his head, puts his sunshades on and exits. When he gets in his car, he puts another call in.

"What it do?" the man answers.

"I can't call it, so my guess is you what's up," Ray returns. "Joe, you know where that nigga Shorty Duce shit?" Ray needs to know. He's thinking, *Fuck what I told Poogie. Shorty Duce just entered in grown folk's territory.*

162

"Yeah, he lives in Hyde Park on the Southside. I think MLK drive. Hold on, let me check." He scrolls thought his phone. "Got it." He gives him the address. Ray stores it in his memory bank.

"Good lookin, G. I'ma throw some'em official your way."

"I'm good. A nigga just wanna get down with yo team, that's all," he informs Ray.

"What team is that, Joe? I ain't got no team."

"C'mon, er' body know you slingin' some'em, G. You and Poo coming up like a mufucka. I just wanna be yo get-down man. I just wanna eat wit y'all."

"My get-down man, huh?"

"Yeah, and I got some official comrades that'a put in work too."

"Nah, nigga you got jokes, but I'ma hold my promise and hit you tomorrow."

"C'mon, G, let's make it do what it do. We can own this fuckin' town. Hell, we can rule the world," he tells Ray.

"From what you heard, I'm already makin' it do what it do and ruling the world without you."

"You know what I mean G. C'mon, we go way back."

"Nigga, I'm only 20. How far could we go back? You's a funny dude, I'm out." Ray disconnects the call. A slight smiles cracks his face as he thinks about what he has in store for the 'hood legend he just hung up wit ... Mac-Ten.

163

CHAPTER 35

Poogie holds his cell phone in his hand, thinking, *How can I do this. I can't … Ok, Andre Smalls, get some sense about yourself. I gotta do it. It's my life or his. I'm not gon' do life and he won't get life. I know he won't get but maybe like 10 to 15 years, that's all. Plus he got a lot of cash flow. He'll get a good lawyer. Shit, he may only get 5 or less and it'll be over.*

He dials the number he never thought he would dial again—but then his cell rings before he can make his call.

"Hey G, where you at?" Ray asks.

"Home, doin' nutten. Where you at?" Poogie asks.

"On my way to the funeral hall to do some finishing touches."

"I wanted to meet up wit' you anyway to get some drinks 'cause shit getting' out of hand in my life," Poogie mutters.

"I feel you on dat there. After I take care of this shit, I'll meet up wit' you, say 12 this afternoon."

"That'a work. I got some shit to take care of too, but that shit is around 12 too. So can we meet at like 3?" Poogie asks.

"3 it is."

"Later," Poogie says.

"Later," Ray returns, then they end their call.

Poogie puts his cell down and takes a shower, then dresses, makes that call, walks out his house to meet Agent Lee to turn over some information that will change his life forever.

CHAPTER 36

Poogie drives up to an old barn off the side of a country road. He gets out of his car and walks into the dusty barn.

"Hello, Poogie," the two FBI agents say in sync.

"Hey look, this ain't me. I can't do this shit no more. Y'all gon' have to do whatever it is you gon' do to me. This shit is real right now."

"Mr. Smalls, we do not have time for games. You signed a contract to work for us, and if you give us something big you will have your life as you know it selling drugs. We all know what you do. We've been watching you. We've been giving you a pass, and you will keep that pass as long as you keep feeding us information on what's going on out there that we don't know about. Now what did you call us down here for? Because I was at home with my family eating and watching a good movie."

Poogie squints his face. "Shit-shit. What have I gotten myself into ...?"

"Mr. Smalls, you're saving your life here."

"I know, man. But I'm killing somebody else's."

"I do not have time for this. What do you have?!" Agent Lee speaks up.

"Shit, fuck!" Poogie holds his head down, then he slowly lifts up. "Ok, here it goes …"

Poogie tells the agents all he knows.

CHAPTER 37

"Mr. Smalls, Poogie—whatever you want to call yourself—it's been a minute. And you have nothing, nothing but that young man's body we found in your car," the agent says, standing in the middle of the old barn with his hands in his coat pockets. "It also looks like to me your living a great life, like money is falling from the sky. Now I need something today. You said six months. Now your word is due. Cash that check," the Agent continues to say.

"Look, I got something big for you but you have to give me time. I know you want it to stick and I know this will stick. I'll give you a drug bust and a murder but you gotta give me more time." Poogie tries to stall for time.

"Would this happen to have anything to do with Mr. Poole?" the agent asks.

"Kinda, why?" Poogie asks.

"We've been watching him. He got a drop on the both of you, so watch yourself. You're sloppy, the same sloppy that got you in this mess. Look, Smalls, I could give a shit about your little drug dealing or whatever you two want to call it. What I need is the kingpin and bodies. That's it. That little shit you and your friend call yourselves doing is light work. The guy that ratted you out is your buddy, one you call Shorty, now I gave you something, now I need something from you," the agent tells him with no chaser.

Poogie is steaming. He's hot about Shorty running his mouth about shit he don't know shit about.

"I just need a little time, man."

"I'm not your man. And I'll give you a little more time, but if nothing turns up soon, you're charged with murder of the young man that we found in the trunk of your car," the agent says with a smirk on his face.

"I got you, no worries over here."

"Oh and Smalls … that Shorty guy, he didn't tell us shit. He tried to tell us you and Mr. Poole were running a high-stakes drug business but he didn't know the deliveries nor the traps. He was worthless. But I gotta give it to'em, he sho tried."

"Did he get off the hook?"

"Hell no, he goes to court soon," he tells Poogie, laughing. "I'll see you soon, and we may have another case for you to work."

"Another case? What you mean another case?" Poogie is baffled.

"We own you now, fucker. Did you not get the memo?"

"I ain't gon' be too many of your fuckers. And what memo?"

"The government owns your black no-good ass," Agent Lee spits coldly.

Poogie looks at him. "You done?"

"For now."

"Good, I got shit to do. And for the record, my name is not James Bond nor will it ever be. Fuck you," Poogie says and gets in his car.

Agent Lee and Leon laugh as they walk to their truck.

CHAPTER 38

A few days after Ray received his wealth of information.

"Bae, I'm goin' to the store. You need anything?" Angie stands at the foot of the stairway, asking Ray as he stands in the middle of the steps wearing only his boxers.

Damn he's so fuckin' fine, I've gotta be the luckiest woman in the world, thank you God, she's thinking as she looks over his fine-ass masculine body. Her eyes stop at the tattoo of her on his chest. A halo hangs over a picture of her with her name printed under her face, *My Little Angel Angie Poole.* He got it done the day after he proposed to her.

"Yeah, pick up some more brewskis. I might not be here when you get back. I gotta go pick up old man P from the airport."

"Who is that?" she questions.

"He's like a father to me. He's from two-up two-down. He makes the best BBQ sauce on the east coast. I used to go to his house during the summer when I was a boy," he explains.

It's so much we don't know about one another. I need to tell him about my sister and father, but now isn't the time, she's thinking.

"Ok, babe, hit me on my hip if you need us," she says with a cat smile, while rubbing her belly and looking up at him.

He looks down without knowing it with a turned up face.

Her smile quickly disappears. "What's wrong, bae?"

"Nothing, boo. My mind just wondered off, that's all."

"Well, can I get a kiss?" she asks.

He steps down four steps, giving her a quick peck on the mouth. "A'ight, drive careful," he tells her, then jogs back up the steps.

"I will. Love you, Ray."

I'm so glad the test said he was the father. He was so happy when he told me he was the father, she walks out the front door thinking to herself while smiling ear to ear.

He gets dressed and goes to the airport to pick up old man P and his wife.

A while later, they get in his car and they talk the whole way to the house. When they pull in the driveway, old man P is in awe. "Man now this is what I call a house, look baby."

"I see P, this is a nice house," his wife comments as they get out the car, collecting their bags.

P leans into Ray's ear. "Boy, you ain't got no land though. You know you need some land wit' this big-ass house. It ain't nutten like spreading them girls' legs in the middle of a big open field," old man P jives as always.

"Man, you crazy. But on the real, a nigga ain't 'bout no bugs. The bedroom is good for me," Ray tells him.

"See, that's what's wrong wit' you youngsters. You gotta learn from us old heads. I can teach you a lot of things. You know they say I'm the best that eva did it. I used ta have them ladies running after me wit' not one flashlight but *fo'*," he tells Ray. They laugh.

"I feel you, man. I'll haveta look into a house wit' a lot of land then," Ray jokes back.

"Let me know. I can hook you up wit' my man in West, VA. Lot of land there."

"Now you pushin' it."

They continue to laugh and joke as they join Mrs. P inside the house. Ray shows them around and they end up in the kitchen.

"Here's the kitchen. Use whateva you need for that famous BBQ," Ray says, rubbing his hands together, licking his lips. He stands and waits for P to get started so he can watch.

"I'on need shit, it's already made."

"What? How you do dat?" Ray asks.

"Yeah, you youngsters not gettin' ahold of my black secret." P's voice becomes serious real fast.

"Ok, you got it, G."

"Who is G? I'm pops or P to you," he corrects Ray.

"You got it, P," Ray corrects himself.

"Man, make yourself at home. You and the misses gon' stay out there in the guest house, or you can stay in here. Whicheva you like."

P looks at his wife and nods his head. "The guest house will work."

Ray laughs and heads to his room thinking, *When I grow up I wanna be just like pops.*

P yells up the steps at Ray. "Ray, I hope you ain't into no illegal shit. I'on wanna see yo ass in the joint when I go to work one day."

"Honey, leave that boy alone. Just because he has all this don't mean he's selling drugs or nothing like that," his wife protests.

"Yeah, that's what they all say," P says, taking his BBQ sauce out the bag.

***

It's six at night and the back yard is full with guests and family members.

"G, these the best ribs a nigga eva had!" Bruce tells him.

"I know. P is the best that eva did it," Ray replies.

"How can you afford all this? This house is dope man," Bruce probes.

"You know I own half of Mr. Rogers and I've been playin' the stocks," he lies to his best friend and his brother.

"Whew, we gotta talk. I got some money I need to unload." Bruce is excited and happy for his man.

Throughout the night, people have been asking Ray how he can afford his house. They've also been congratulating him on his engagement. They all party and drink all night, living it up.

"This engagement party is beautiful. You two really went out," Bruce's grandmother tells Ray. I wish your mother could be here to see it."

"Fuck that bird bitch!" Ray spits venom.

He still hasn't forgiven her for taking Bruce's father. She and Bruce's mother were best friends. Just like Bruce's mother, Ray's mother became an addict from the product that Bruce's father was selling. Ray feels his mother chose her friend's man over her own son. He hates Bruce's father and he hated his own mother more. He feels like she should've been stronger, and because of Fred (Bruce's father), she sent Ray to live with his aunt who died the day after Ray graduated. She had breast cancer. But it was as if she hung on until she saw him walk across the stage, receiving his high school diploma. Ray's blood father was a real G. He died in a gangsta war. He went out a true G. The 'hood still bleeds his name. Ray holds his rep and shines his blood.

"Don't say that. That woman's your blood," Bruce's grandmother says to him.

"That's where you're wrong. The only blood that I have is the blood of a G," he tells her, pointing to his arm that reads: *Ray Poole Sr. the best that eva did it!*

Seeing she has no chance of winning, she changes the subject. "You win, you're grown. Question for ya: Who is that fine man on the grill?"

"That's old man P and that lovely lady standing over there"—he points across the yard—"is his wife of 25 years."

"You can't blame an old lady for trying, can you? *Umph*, he's fine as hell," she says, walking off.

"And you old as hell tryna holla at niggas, now that's some nasty shit," Ray frowns, making his whole body quiver.

"You're neva to old," a male's voice utters from behind.

Ray turns around. "What up, man? I thought you couldn't make it." He gives Poogie a gangsta tap.

"Nigga you know I wasn't gon' miss this shit. I just think you should wait a little longer, that's all."

"Everything that looks like a duck ain't always a duck, you feel me?" Ray expresses.

"Like a tight rubber. Sometimes you gotta tell'em what they wanna hear to keep they mouth shut," Poogie relates, downing a cold one.

"That you ain't neva lied about," Ray tells him, not letting his right hand know what his left is really up to.

"Where that nigga Bruce?" Poogie is asking, looking around.

"He around here somewhere. I just saw him and Angie over by the grill talkin'."

Now Ray is curious as he looks around. He doesn't see either one of them. He brushes it off, continuing to talk to his boy, knowing what he has in store for the both of them.

CHAPTER 39

It's dawn. The sun is on the rise, painting a picture of bright orange half-covered by the clouds. It seems like it's going to be a scorcher. Ray enjoyed his weekend and all of the guests that attended his engagement cookout. He allowed it to take place at his house because he sold it one week ago. The buyers are moving in next week. He never wanted anyone to know where he shits or lays his head. No one but Poogie knows that he just purchased a condo in Indi. He made a mint off the sale of his house because of the renovations. He bought the house just to fix it up and flip it, and it work out well for him.

Everything is going as planned in his life. Well not everything. He sits back thinking about all the shit that has transpired over the last few months.

Who says thugs don't cry? The more money you make, the more problems. Niggas think this life is sweet, they just don't know; it's more blood, lies, and tears than the price of fame should allow. Sometimes I wish I was still livin' in da Wild Hunnids working fo' old man Roger. Life was easy then, he continues to think as he gets out his car. He's parked outside his boy Bruce's house. His legs feel like they're lifting a ton of bricks as he makes his way up the long stairway to the front door. Even his arms feel heavy as he lifts his hand to ring the doorbell.

Ding dong!

Bruce looks out the sliding glass peephole. "What up, G!" he shouts, unlocking the door for his main man.

"You, nigga," Ray returns, giving him some dap.

"Come in. Why you standing out there like you some salesman and shit? What brings my main man across the way this fuckin' early in the morning?"

"I can't come holla at my mans and shit?"

"Fa' sho, fa' sho. I ain't doing shit but studying some plays for the game. Man, my brain is fried. I been up all night, but I can make time fa' my man no madda what time it is," Bruce says, walking towards his bar.

"You doin' your homework, huh?"

"You already know. Have a seat. You gon' make a nigga's house poor. You act like dis not your home too. You know what's mines is yours, and that there is real talk. Well, not everything, not my girl," Bruce laughs, scooping some ice out the ice pale, dropping cubes in the glass.

"Make yo house poor, huh? I ain't heard that shit since aunt Wendy died." Ray's heart starts pumping. "Me and you have shared a lot of things, but one thing you're right about, we can't share our women."

"Now that there wouldn't work. What you drinking dis early, some OJ?"

"Hell nah, you know how I do it. That Henny, even if it is early in da muthafuckin' AM," Ray spits.

"Yep, that would be yo get down," Bruce returns with his back turned, pouring Ray's drink.

"Look, man. It's something I need to holla at you about," Ray informs.

"Then holla, playa. What's poppin'?" Bruce says as he now pours himself something to drink.

Ray pulls his Desert Eagle out from his hoodie pocket. He raises his gun, aiming at Bruce's head. He takes about five steps toward him.

Bloc! Bloc! Bloc! Bloc! is the sound that rings throughout the house. Poor Bruce's brains splatter all over the bar. He didn't even see it coming.

Ray lowers his banger to his side, walking up to his man, his best friend, his brother. He looks down at his body and allows tears to drop from his eyes.

He loves Bruce so much but as a gangsta he has to stick to the code.

Death before Dishonor.

After about five minutes of standing over his man's lifeless body, he pulls his thoughts together. "What happened?

You used to be platinum. Dis new game you got in done ... turned you soft. Outta all the bitches, why mines?" Ray speaks his peace, kisses his two fingers then throws them in the air. "Rest in peace, my man."

He pulls his hoodie over his head, placing his banger in his oversized pocket. Leaves, jumps in his car and speeds off.

***

The ride back to Illinois seemed long. Lots of memories float about. Ray feels like he just lost his soul.

Niggas know my get-down so why test the waters? They should know if they fuck wit' me, I'ma make them pay taxes, he's thinking, sitting behind the wheel of his hooptie.

Three hours later he pulls up to the spot where he told Angie to meet him. It's 12 noon. The day is still long. The sun is bright yellow, blazing fire. Ray puts his car in park and gets out.

Angie steps out her car.

"Bae, why you wanna meet back here? All these abandoned buildings. It's kinda creepy."

"I know, I'm sorry boo, but Five-O is hot on my heels right now."

"What?! Why?! Did they follow you here?" she asks, looking around.

Moving closer to her with his right hand resting on his banger inside his pocket, he says, "Boo, why you had to go and fuck my man?"

"What?! Boy, you trippin'. What man you talkin 'bout?"

"If you have to ask me, then you already know. But to make myself clear, I'm talkin 'bout my man Bruce."

"Bruce? I didn't mess with no Bruce. He fucks wit' my—"

Bloc! Bloc!

Two in her chest, cutting her windpipe off. Her head hits the dirt like a stack of bricks. He hovers over her body. Her eyes are still open, her mouth as well. He rips her skirt, pulls her thong to the side, sticks his steaming hot banger in her pussy and allows his trigger finger to do the talking.

Bloc!

"Tricks are for kids. No bastards! Rest in peace, shawdy. Tell your lover Bruce I said hi when you see'em. Oh, ask Jesus to forgive me of my sins," he whispers.

Then like a vampire he places his dark shades over his bloodshot eyes and rides out.

***

A few minutes later Ray rolls up to Shorty Duce's joint, but Shorty is outside with Bey washing his car. His neighbors are sitting on their porch, husband wife and two teen boys.

185

Ray scans the area for more witnesses. He sees none. Pulling into Shorty Duce's driveway, he throws his car in park, quickly hops out, .40 in hand—*Bloc! Bloc! Bloc! Bloc!*

He puts one in Shorty's head and chest. Bey catches one in her leg and one straight to her right eyeball, sending both of them to glory. Shorty's neighbors stare in dismay. They are stuck, as they don't know what to do. They're just stuck.

Ray reaches for his .50 Glock that's pressed against his hip bone. He points it their way. *Bloc, bloc, bloc, bloc, bloc, bloc!*

He sprays the onlookers, all of them down but one of the teens. He pumps lead in his back. He tried to escape death but Ray's sharp shooting skills outrun him this day. Ray runs over to make sure no one is breathing.

The husband flinches. *Bloc!* Total blackout.

"Sorry, wrong place wrong time." Ray feels he did them dirty. Not wanting to do them sticky, he runs to his car, grabs a few stacks, goes back to the victim's yard, drops ten on the father's body. "For the funerals," he whispers, then scans his surroundings. No more eyes that he can see. He runs back to Shorty's driveway. Like a thief in the night he's extinct.

***

"It's five and the sun is still hot. It seems like it's gotten hotter as he turns the corner where Mac-Ten awaits him. Ray call's Mac-Ten's name, leaning out his car window. Mac sees its Ray. He waves his hands, gesturing for him to pull up beside him. Locked and loaded, Ray pulls up to him. Mac is leaning comfortably on the hood of his car.

Bloc!

Mac crumples over from the heat he's feeling in his stomach. Holding his stomach, he looks up at Ray. *Bloc!* Ray strikes again, sending a bullet through his heart.

Ray rolls his window back up and peels out.

As he drives down highway 94, he starts winding down. His heart slows down and his palms start to dry off. He's tired from all the driving; he's tired of the mayhem. He just wants to take a hot shower, then go into a deep sleep.

He pulls up to an abounded house, parks, gets out, raises the garage door where his all-white BMW awaits his arrival. Grabbing a can full of gas, he dowses the hooptie. He goes back into the garage, undresses, pours water from a jug into a bucket, giving himself a bird bath. He changes his clothes, puts the old clothes in a plastic bag and throws them into the old car. He gets into his BMW, starts it and pulls out a Molotov cocktail bomb, lights the end of it and throws it inside the old hooptie. He drives off, watching it go up in flames in his rearview mirror.

When he's home, he grabs his throw-away and calls Poogie.

"What up, G? We good, you good?" Poogie greets.

"Why wouldn't we be? You already know the blood I bleed," Ray tells him.

"True gangsta blood, no doubt." Poogie is kind of panicking.

"True indeed. Look, I'm tired. I'ma get some rest. I'll holla at you lata. I gotta get ready for the movers to come tonight."

"That's right, you coming my way. You movin' ta Indi, my nigga. We gon' keep slums in the city?" Poogie questions.

"Nah man, we gon' turn up the city. We comin' out full force."

"I'm wit' you on dat, partna."

They end their call and Ray goes to the bedroom, undresses, steps into the hot shower. He rests his forehead against the wall, allowing the hot water to take over his sexy body. Lathering his rag, spreading suds all over his body. He sits on the marble slab, rinsing off the suds. Ray starts thinking about all the people he bodied. Tears fall one after another. He's already missing his girl and his boy. He's wondering how he allowed this to happen. He vows to never allow anyone else to penetrate his heart, his emotions. Standing up, his mind erases total memory of it all.

"I'm gon' turn it up. I have no love ones to get in my way. Niggas ain't got shit they can hold over my head. I'm rollin' full gangsta, me against the world," he utters out loud, as he dries his tears.

CHAPTER 40

The news of all the murders sang though the media waves.
They're having a field day with all the drama and mayhem.
The police are not sure if the murders are connected but
one thing is for sure, Ray has them working instead of
eating doughnuts and drinking coffee. They have no witnesses. The one thing that is hurting them is the innocent
teen boys that were shot. Why would someone kill children,
and why would someone shoot a child in the back ... why?

The city is in an up roar. They want answers, and
they want them now. Somebody has to pay. They also can't
understand who would kill an up and coming great basketball superstar. Bruce was pulling the Bulls through their bad
time. This is all people are hearing over the airwaves, and no
one is talking about Angie the saleswoman, or Shorty Duce
the thug. They are only concerned about the white family
and the basketball star.

Ray pays a visit to Bruce's grandmother and they sit at the kitchen table.

"I'm so sorry about all of this," Ray tells her. "I'll pay for it all ... everything. Whateva you need, you say so."

He doesn't have to pay for the funeral because the NBA has taken care of it all, she informs him. Ray shows much love by giving her money anyway to help with anything else she may need. Bruce's grandmother is holding the funeral off until Ray buries Angie. She tells him it's just too much for her right now. They sit and talk about old times. They laugh and laugh, then she turns to Ray.

"Ray, I have a surprise for you. I have someone I want you to meet. I know Bruce was going to tell you about her, or should I say, *them*, but he was waiting for the right time to come."

"Not now, I just don't feel like it. I got too much going on in my life. Nothing at this point would be a surprise, nothing."

"But Ray …"

"I just don't want to, but when all this is over I will meet anyone you want me to, how about that?"

"It's going to have to be ok."

"Good. If you need anything, you have my number. I love you, Grandma Brenda." Ray hugs her around her neck.

"I love you too," she tells him.

They hug for a long time. "I'm so sorry that it has to be

this way," he tells her.

She breaks their embrace and eyeballs him. "Boy, you don't have to apologize to me. This is not your fault. Whoeva did this to'em, they gon' pay. God knows who did it. Even if the police neva find out, the man upstairs already knows. Whoeva did this thinks they got away but they would rather deal with the police than God, trust me on that one."

Ray holds his head down, feeling the guilt that's weighting his shoulders. He says nothing more, just walks out her door.

CHAPTER 41

"G, them niggas that was hot on your trail, them was some niggas from the West Side, some of Youngbleed's goons," Poogie informs Ray over the phone.

"Youngbleed's boys? Now tell me why would they be on my tail, Poo. 'Cause we both know I'on have shit ta do wit' dat nigga's murder. Dat there ain't my rap ta take," Ray says, placing his hand on his head confused.

"I know, but for some reason they think it was you," Poogie says with a smile.

"Oh, I guess we look alike in black hoodies, huh?" Ray spits, letting him know he knows it was him. "G, you gotta start coming correct. You gettin' sloppy as hell. I mean really sloppy. Yo work ain't bulletproof like it used ta be. Look at Bruce's father. You ain't hear shit, did you? Nutten. But this here is some rat ass fucked up punk nigga shit. I smell a true rat lurking. This is how it works, huh? You tell me, Poo, *tell me!*" Ray's outraged so he rants.

Poogie remains silent with a smile on his face.

"Look G, that's the word right now in them streets."
Ray pauses for 10 seconds, stands and paces the floor. "I
can't have people breathing down my back like this. I can't
make no bread fuckin' around wit' stupid shit like dis, so
as you know it 5-0 gon' be beating down my door over
somebody else's sloppy ass work. Dat shit happened to my
brother Curt-Bone, and I sho nuff ain't gon' let dat shit
happen to me. I ain't doing time fo' no man that bleeds the
same blood as me. I take my own rap, no one else's. Poo, get
yo life together. These streets breathe rumors, know that.
And it's not just about me and Youngbleed. Get this shit
right, G. Get it right. I'm ghost," Ray spits, ending their call.

Poogie sits in his chair laughing like life is a cat and
mouse game 'cause he's the one eating the cheese.

CHAPTER 42

Everyone is gathered at Angie's funeral. Ray is seated in the front row with her mother and her mother's husband. Poogie is seated beside Ray. They're both sitting in silence while many people view Angie's body. Ray is in deep thought about him and Angie and how good she made him feel her soft skin. The conversations they would have and all the fun he had with her. He loves her so much but Death before Dishonor is the code he has to live by, no matter who it is. His heart is still broken. This is one of the hardest days to come. He still has Bruce's funeral to attend.

His thoughts are broken from the feeling of his cell vibrating against his hip. "Hello?" he answers the unfamiliar number.

"Hello, Mr. Poole, please."

"This me."

"This is Doctor Banger. That test I read you the other day was incorrect. My receptionist got the names mixed up.

Somehow she typed the results in under the wrong Green. Mr. Poole, what I am trying to tell you is that she made a big mistake." Ray raises to his feet. Poogie looks up at him like what the fuck is getting ready to go down.

"So what you saying?"

"Mr. Poole, I'm sorry but you are 99% the father of the child that Ms. Angie Green is carrying. Sir, you are the baby's father!" He is excited to deliver the news. Ray's last words the day he talked to him has been haunting him every night.

"What?! What you sayin?" Ray's voice reaches a high level.

"G, what's up?" Poogie stands.

Ray moves his feet fast toward the lobby of the church, holding his cell to his ear with Poogie on his heels.

"Doc, you there?" Ray adds.

"I'm still here. Aren't you happy the baby is yours?" the doctor repeats.

"How could she make a mistake like dat?!"

"We ran tests on two Ms. Greens in my office that very same day and both of their first names begin with an A so she got them mixed up. But she is no longer employed here, needless to say."

"Doc ..."

Ray cuts himself short as he becomes face to face with a woman that looks exactly like the love of his life. Poogie is standing behind him thinking, *I know we ain't being Punk'd or some'em, or did she rise from the dead.*

"Who are you?" Ray is puzzled right now because he knows he just left out the main hall of the church and Angie's body was laying stiff in a pine box.

"I should be asking you that. So who are you?" she returns.

"I'm Ray, Angie's man."

"So you're Ray ... I heard so much about you. Hell, I should have known right off who you was from all the pictures he has around the house of you and him." She starts crying.

"What?! Who in the hell are you? What pictures, whose house?" Ray asks as Poogie stands beside him grilling her.

"I'm sorry, I miss him so much. How could anyone want ta kill him like that? He left me carrying his child. He said he was going to tell you that we was going to get married, but me and my twin sister didn't see eye to eye on most things so you may not have known about me. I don't get along with my mother and Angie very well. I love her and my father does too. But ... but ... oh my God, they're both gone, why God!" she is yelling and crying.

"Her sister?! Her sister?! Her twin?!" Ray yells, falling to his knees balling. "What have I done? What?!" he cries out, looking at the ceiling. "Oh God!" He starts thinking about what Bruce said before he killed him, how Bruce's grandmother tried to tell him about her, how she wanted him to meet her, how Angie tried to tell him about her before he pulled the deadly trigger.

People start coming out to see what's going on. Poogie helps his man up, he wants to get him out the church so he can get some fresh air. Ray is leaning on Poogie's shoulder, struggling to walk. They exit through the double doors only to be met by Chicago's finest, the CPD.

CHAPTER 43

"Raymond Poole, you have a visit," a C.O. of the Chicago city jail yells out.

Ray picks himself up and makes his way to the visiting booth the C.O. assigns him. He picks up the rusty yellowish handset.

"Hey, G," Poogie voices, sitting on the other side of freedom.

"Hey G, what up," Ray says.

"You man, how you holding?"

"I'm holding, tryna get the fuck outta here."

"What's the bond?"

"None. They say I'm a flight risk."

"G, you gotta be kiddin'."

"It's ok, my lawyer got this," Ray tells him, looking him in his eyes.

"What they saying?"

"They tryna hit a nigga wit' first degree for Youngbleed."

"What? You didn't do that shit."

"Me and you know dat on the real. These hot ass crackas, they don't seem to know this. They say they got an eye witness and shit," Ray spits, raising one eyebrow.

"G, this here is fucked up."

"Really it is," Ray comes back with his eyebrow still raised.

"We gotta find out who the witness is," Poogie shoots with a nervousness in his voice.

"I think we already know who he is," Ray boldly says. "Poo, this here is my town. Don't shit get past me. This one was just too late. I know you had to do what you had to do. G, I really forgive you. I neva thought it would be you that put me here, but this one is on me. See, my brother said *trust no man* but I put my guard down, so here I lie," he says in a settled tone.

Poogie looks at him, thinking quickly. "Sorry man, them pigs was in my shit, talking 'bout life man. I can't do life, G. I can't. I thought you would get off with no priors."

"All you had to do was tell me you smoked little man and his girl, I would've helped you get out that shit."

"How you know it was me?" Poogie asks.

"My gut, and you confirmed it just now," Ray tells him with a tear running down one eye.

Those were the last words from Ray's mouth to Poogie. Ray presses his hand against the window, then walks away.

Poogie sits for about five minutes holding the receiver, dropping tears before the C.O. tells him he has to go.

He takes a long walk to his car, feeling like he's done the worst thing any man could do. But he did. It was a choice he took.

CHAPTER 44

One Week Later

Poogie, Big C and Kim are on a back road waiting for the red light to turn green. Big C suggests this route to avoid traffic.

They pull out some trees as they rock to the sounds of Yo Gotti.

"G, that show was dope. I mean Jay-Z was doing his thing. For that nigga to be so old, he still got it."

He was, but B she was doing her thing. I love that bitch. She got it going on," Kim says, sitting in the passenger seat.

"It was a'ight," Big C lets out as he sits behind Poogie.

The light turns green.

"G, pull over right here. I gotta piss," Big C lets out.

"G, yo ass always gotta piss. Damn, I'm tryna get home," Poogie says, looking at Kim with lust in his eyes.

"Just pull yo punk ass over."

Poogie pulls over to the curb. Big C opens the door. He pulls his 9mm pistol out. He puts the cold steel to Poogie's temple.

"Man! What you doing? Not in front my girl. Nah man, not like this!" Poogie whines.

"I ain't yo girl. I'on fuck wit Rats," Kim lets out as she opens the door, stepping into the dark.

"Who sent you? Why you doing this, we boys G!" Poogie continues to whine.

"Nobody sent me. This here is business for my little bro and my man Ray, you rat ass nigga."

Poogie steps on the gas, the car takes off. Big C's side of the door is still open. His body jerks back, he gains control and—*Bloc!* Poogie's head jerks forward, his foot presses hard on the gas. Big C looks around thinking, *Should I jump?* But the car is out of control. He manages to put the gun in his jacket, then he says a quick prayer as he jumps for safety.

EPILOGUE

"Raymond Poole, you have a legal."

"What my lawyer want? He wasn't due til next week," Ray says to one of the guys he's playing bones with.

He makes his way to the visit room.

"Hello, Raymond," his attorney says as Ray takes a seat.

"Hello," Ray returns with a puzzled look on his face.

"I have good news and bad. Which one first?"

"Good," Ray tells him, leaning back in his chair.

"You're being released."

"What?!"

"Yes, the witness was murdered."

"Well that is good news, but they're not going to try and say I killed the witness, are they?" Ray asks.

"No, not that I've heard."

"Now, that *issss* good news!" Ray barks, cracking a smile, knowing his boy Big C took care of his problem.

But he knew he would once Carman told him that Poogie killed his little brother and the reason he got away with it was because he is working for the Feds. He can always depend on Carman to come through.

"Now here is the bad news: The judge will not be back to sign the paperwork for two weeks, and the higher judge will not be back for another three weeks, so you will have to be in here for two more weeks."

"I can handle that."

"They will have to pay you for each day you stay from this date on. It will be $100 a day," his attorney explains.

"Thanks, man."

They shake hands and part. Ray walks back to his pod, smiling and thinking, *You rat-ass nigga, I win. Rats never win. They never win, bitch-ass nigga and bitches. All of 'em can go where Poogie is—straight to HELL!*

Text **JORDAN** to **77948**

And stay updated on all of Jordan Belcher Presents' *newest releases, free giveaways,* and *special promotions!*

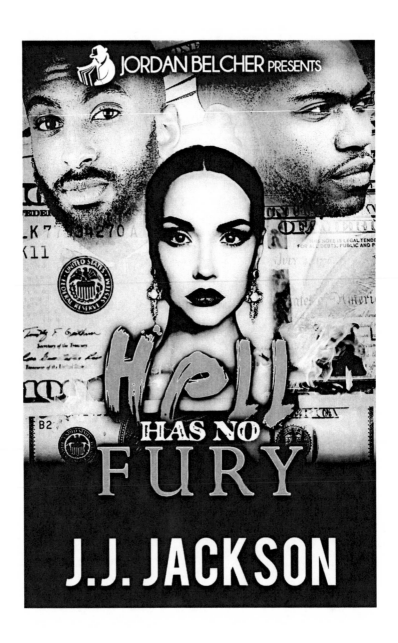

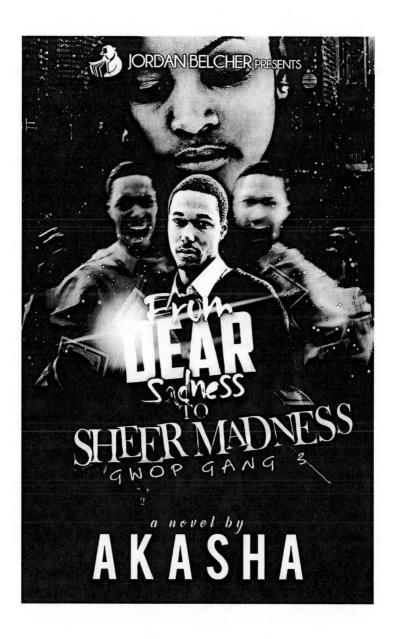